The Bear Who Wouldn't Leave

J.H. Moncrieff

D1602625

DeathZone Books, Ltd.
www.deathzonebooks.com

The Bear Who Wouldn't Leave
Copyright @ 2015 by J.H. Moncrieff
Print ISBN: 978-0-9877129-2-9
Digital ISBN: 978-0-9877129-1-2

Editing by Don D'Auria

Cover Art by Kelly Martin
www.kam.design/book-covers

Formatting by Jacob Hammer

Dedication

For Chris and Dee Dee, who made it happen.

Chapter One

It was the ugliest thing I'd ever seen.

"I don't want it," I said, pushing it back at my mother.

"Now, Josh—be nice. This was your father's when he was a child, and he really wants you to have it."

I folded my arms across my chest as she continued to shove the toy at me. "He's *not* my father."

My father had died two years ago, when I was only eight. Mom said his heart stopped, which sounded terrifying. How did a person's heart just…stop? Dad's heart quit working while he was sleeping, so for a year I didn't want to go to bed. I was afraid the same thing would happen to me.

The only thing I liked less than the ugly toy was Michael, my new stepfather. Oh, he seemed nice enough, I guess, but there was something about him that gave me the creeps. Maybe it was the way his smile never reached his eyes. Or the times I'd caught him staring at me when he thought I wasn't looking. I couldn't understand how Mom could love someone like that. My real dad had been so nice. His eyes had crinkled at the corners when he laughed, and he laughed *a lot*. Michael hardly ever laughed, and when he did, it made me shiver.

Mom sighed. She tried to hide it, but I noticed her lower lip was trembling. Again. She cried at anything these days, even those sappy commercials about starving kids in the Sudan, wherever that was. "He's trying, Josh. Can't you be a little nicer to him? It would mean a lot to me."

I didn't want to see her cry again, so I said sure, I would be nicer. She looked relieved as she pressed the toy into my arms and thanked me. Then she asked me what I would like for dinner, which was a treat. Lately we'd only had Michael's requests, and Michael wanted weird things like steamed spinach and broccoli soup. What kind of person actually likes broccoli?

She seemed a bit troubled when I requested macaroni and cheese— she was probably worried Michael wouldn't like it. She hurried to the kitchen, leaving me alone with the bear.

A teddy bear. Who gives a ten-year-old boy a teddy bear? I was into The Incredible Hulk and riding my bike. A teddy bear was a little kid's toy.

I turned the bear over in my hands. Even its fur felt nasty, matted and a bit greasy. I guess it was supposed to be a panda, even though it wasn't like any panda I'd ever seen. Its body was mostly black, and it had black patches over both eyes. Around its neck was a tattered yellow ribbon.

Its eyes were beady, the kind of eyes you see in scary cartoon paintings—the type that seem to follow you around. But the worst was its mouth. It was curled into a vicious snarl so you could see its teeth, and it had huge fangs. What kind of teddy bear has fangs? Nothing about it was soft or cuddly. It was so stiff it was like a piece of wood in my arms.

The longer I held the bear, the spookier it was. I could swear it was staring back at me, but that was crazy—it was only a toy. It was my imagination playing tricks on me, just like how I was always sure someone was chasing me whenever I ran upstairs from the basement.

All I knew was that I wanted to put as much space between it and me as possible. I threw it in my closet, under a pile of dirty clothes that smelled so bad even Mom wouldn't go near them. She might be able to make me take the bear, but she couldn't force me to play with it.

I went outside to join my friends and forgot all about the bear—until it was time for bed.

Chapter Two

The second I stepped into my room, I could tell something wasn't right. It felt like someone was already inside, waiting for me, but I had no brothers or sisters and my friends had gone home.

Suddenly, for some reason I couldn't understand, I was scared. I'd been about to turn on the light, but I had this feeling I shouldn't.

"Hello?" I said, feeling silly. I had no idea who I was saying hello to, but I really hoped no one would answer me. No one did.

Before I could stop myself, I flicked on the light. What I saw made me jump. The ugly bear was on my bed! It seemed to be looking at me, its snout twisted into a snarl. I ran to the living room as fast as I could.

My mother glanced up from the television in surprise. "Josh, what are you still doing up? I thought we agreed it was time for you to go to bed."

Michael wasn't surprised to see me. If anything, he seemed happy. He had a weird smirk on his face that I didn't like at all.

"Did you go in my room?" I was asking them both, but my question was really for him.

"Now, Josh, don't be silly. Why would we go in your room?" Mom asked, but I ignored her. I was still glaring at Michael, who was staring right back at me.

"Why do you think someone's been in your room?" he asked,

smooth as silk. I noticed he didn't deny it.

"The bear is on my bed! Someone put him there."

"What bear? What on earth are you talking about?" I could tell from the tone of Mom's voice that she was confused, but she was beginning to get upset too. She always could pick up on my thoughts better than anyone else, and I was breathing so hard she could probably hear it.

Michael patted her leg. "It's nothing to get upset about, Eileen. I believe Josh is referring to the teddy bear I gave him. Isn't that right, Josh?"

He smiled, but I imagined that behind his curved lips, he had sharp white fangs like his bear. It was easy enough to believe.

"Did you put him on my bed?" I demanded. I was so angry I could spit, but plenty scared too.

"If he's on your bed, I'm sure you put him there. You probably got busy playing and forgot."

That's the other thing I didn't like about Michael. He talked to me like I was a moron instead of a kid. As if I had been stupid enough to leave that bear on my bed and then forget about it. And the worst part was, I could tell he didn't believe it. I could see it in his face—he knew *exactly* how the bear got there.

"You *did* put him there!"

"Now, honey, I'm not sure what's going on," Mom said, looking warily from Michael to me and back again, "but I'm sure Michael's right—you just forgot."

"I didn't forget!" I was close to screaming now. I could feel my face getting hot.

"Okay, okay." She walked over to me and put her hand on my shoulder. For a second, I was tempted to push her away, but that would have hurt her feelings, and it wasn't her fault Michael had given me that creepy bear. But it *was* her fault that Michael was in our lives to start with. A part of me hated her for that. I pulled away.

She bent down to look into my eyes. "Where did you leave the bear?"

"In my closet. It was under some clothes. There's no way I forgot and put it on my bed."

Mom straightened. Disappointment was written all over her face. I could tell she was unhappy about where I'd left Michael's gift.,.

We both were startled when my stepfather laughed. "Well, that explains it. A closet is no place for a bear. I'm sure Edgar walked out of there and got on the bed himself."

My mouth dropped open, but Mom responded before I could say anything. "That's not funny. Children have very active imaginations, and you have to be careful what you say to them. Talking like that will give him nightmares."

"I'm not a child!" I yelled. I was sick and tired of everyone babying me and acting like I was a little kid. If anything, I understood more than they did. How could they not see that bear was creepy?

"Exactly. He's not a child, Eileen. He isn't scared of my little teddy bear—are you, Josh? The boy knows I'm just kidding around."

They both waited for my response. Mom still seemed concerned, but hesitant, perhaps wondering if this was worth making a big deal over. The only people who appeared to be upset by this conversation were the two of us. Michael continued to smile, showing off his shark-like teeth.

As for me, I was in a tough spot. If I wanted to be treated like a big boy—and I did—I could hardly admit that I was scared of a little teddy bear. More than anything, I wished for a moment alone with my mother.

I wished I could tell her that there was no way I could sleep in that room with Edgar. (Who names a teddy bear *Edgar*, anyway? How creepy is that?) But if I admitted it in front of Michael, I'd never hear the end of it. He'd been nicer when he was just dating my mother. Now that they were married, I was getting the idea that he was the kind of person who said cruel things and then claimed he was only "teasing."

"Well, it's getting late," Michael said in a jovial tone, thumping his hand on the armrest. "Why don't I tuck you in?"

Panicked, I met my mother's eyes with my best pleading expression. She immediately understood.

"That's not necessary, honey. He's ten years old. He's totally capable of putting himself to bed."

"Oh, I don't mind. It's no trouble. Come on, Josh. Let's go." Michael held out his hand, and I had to take it if I didn't want to seem rude. His unspoken message was clear—if I was going to act like a child, he was going to treat me like one. His skin was rough against mine, and in that moment, I hated him with a ferocity that spooked me.

Somehow it was even worse to see Edgar waiting on my bed when Michael was beside me. They were both on the same team, and I was the odd one out. I knew it was crazy to think that about a teddy bear, but that was the way it felt.

"Ah, that's perfect. See how happy the little guy is. That's definitely the spot for him," Michael said, and he was right. The bear *did* seem happier. Viewed from this perspective, his snarling muzzle could have been a smile. I knew then that Michael had put him on my bed, but I wondered how he'd known where to search. Maybe when he was a kid, he'd kept Edgar in the closet too.

Michael wouldn't let go of my hand until we reached the bed. He loomed over me, waiting, while I crawled beneath the covers, careful not to touch the bear. I prayed Michael wouldn't read me a bedtime story. I didn't think I could handle that, but I needn't have worried. He bent down so his face was close to mine, so close our noses were almost touching. *Oh God, is he going to give me a goodnight kiss?* It took every bit of willpower I had not to pull the covers over my face. If I were rude to him, Mom would never let me hear the end of it.

"Listen, kid, I know you don't like me, and you're not exactly my choice for son of the year either."

I was shocked by his words, and suddenly frightened. This was the first time my stepfather had told me how he really felt. The cheerful tone he used around my mother had been replaced by a threatening growl.

"But we're stuck with each other, and if we can't be father and son, we can at least try to get along and maybe be friends, okay?"

I cringed back into my pillow in an attempt to put a little more space between his face and mine. Was he crazy? I would never think of him as a friend, ever.

Satisfied by my response, or maybe just by my fear, Michael straightened. "Edgar means a lot to me, so I hope you treat him well. If you don't…well…let's just say I'll know."

He walked to my door and shut off the light, leaving me in the dark.

Chapter Three

Scuttling to the far side of the bed, I pulled the covers to my chin and closed my eyes. I tried not to think about Edgar sitting on the other side of my pillow, leering into the dark. In a funny way Michael had helped distract me, because he'd given me a lot of other stuff to think about.

A tear formed in the corner of my eye and trickled over the bridge of my nose onto my pillow. My heart ached for my dad. Dad would never have let anyone talk to me like that, and if he'd still been around, Mom wouldn't have looked twice at Michael. In a weird way, she'd actually met Michael through Dad—Michael owned the funeral home where we'd held Dad's service. Even then, I hadn't liked him. He'd followed Mom around, asking too many questions, and whenever she'd cried and he'd tried to comfort her, his hugs had lasted a little too long.

But it still hurt to know he didn't like me. No grown-up had ever said anything like that to me before, and as I thought about it, the tears came faster. I buried my face in the pillow so Michael wouldn't hear, wouldn't know how much his words had bugged me. And then something happened that made me stop feeling sorry for myself.

Something touched the back of my neck.

I bolted upright with a screech, slapping wildly at my bare skin. There was nothing there, but as I sat up, I'd felt something fall over to rest against my hip. I was pretty sure I knew what it was.

Flicking on the lamp, I covered my eyes until they stopped stinging. And then I sat that way for a moment longer. I knew what I'd find when I took my hand away. I knew, but I didn't want to see it.

Don't be silly. It's only a toy, and toys can't touch you. You were moving, and he fell against you. That's all.

I peeked through two fingers and there he was. Edgar was resting against my side like he was snuggled in for the night.

I could have sworn that damn bear was grinning at me.

Sliding out of bed, I pinched one of his ears and ran with him to the closet. This time I buried him even deeper under the pile of clothes, and shoved the whole mess far to the back. Michael would have to work harder to find him this time.

Only when Edgar was safely in the closet could I get back in bed, but I kept the light on. No matter how tightly I gathered the blankets around me, I couldn't get warm.

Edgar stayed in the closet for two days, and I was finally able to sleep again. Maybe everything had been my imagination after all. Even Michael acted like nothing had happened between us, like he hadn't said that terrible thing about not wanting me for a son. He seemed to be in an extra good mood. He cooked pancakes for breakfast, making sure my bacon was crispy, just the way I liked it. The day after he gave me the bear, he came home with a bouquet of yellow roses for my mom. Yellow roses were her favorite, and she was so happy I decided it was only right that I try to be happy too. She'd been so sad after Dad died—why wreck her one little bit of joy? I tried not to think that Michael had probably taken the roses from someone else's coffin.

On the third day, I had a friend over to play. His name was Sean. He wasn't my best friend—that would be Tom, but Tom had been acting weird since my father died. He'd really loved my dad, who used to take us both on fishing and camping trips. Mom said Tom probably didn't know what to say to me, but that made no sense. He didn't have to say anything in order to come over and play. He only had to show up.

If Tom wasn't around, I hung out with Sean. I liked Sean okay, but I didn't ask him over much because my mother didn't approve of what she called "his language." I think that was because Sean tended to swear. A lot.

"Holy Judith, Mother of Hell," Sean cried when he walked into my room. (Most of Sean's swears didn't make any sense.) "What in the blazing ass is this?"

I had no idea what he was talking about, but when I saw he was pointing to my bed, I instantly understood. It was Edgar, glaring at me from my own pillow. The flesh on my arms tightened into goose bumps, and I suppressed a shudder.

"You're sleeping with fricking teddy bears now?" Sean's eyes gleamed, and I knew he thought he'd hit the kids' version of a jackpot—something he could use to tease and embarrass me for the rest of my life.

"No, it's a dumb joke of my stepfather's," I said. Thankfully, my pajama top was still lying on the bed. I threw it over Edgar and gathered it around the bear, scooping up the top into a makeshift bag that I threw into my closet. Sean watched me with curiosity.

"What was that about?" he asked.

I shrugged. "I don't like to touch it, that's all. I don't like the way it feels."

"Can't blame you there. That is one ugly-ass bear."

I had a great time with Sean that afternoon. He used almost every toy I had, and even some stuff that wasn't toys, to construct the biggest Matchbox track of all time. The track went around and around my room, guiding the little cars through dominos and a running shoe and even Darth Vader. Even though it was the most fun I'd had in a long time, I was eager for Sean to leave. Finally I pleaded a stomachache so he wouldn't invite himself over for dinner, as he often did. I wanted to talk to my mom before Michael got home. Usually they were home from work around the same time, but today was Saturday and Michael had a funeral, so I'd be able to talk to her in private.

"Is it a stabbing pain or an ache?" Mom asked once Sean had left, and for a moment I was confused. Then I realized my friend must have told her about my "stomachache" on the way out.

I shrugged. "Just an ache, I guess."

She touched my forehead, feeling for fever. It usually drove me crazy when she was overprotective, but now I was grateful for the attention. It had been so long since I'd had her all to myself.

"Why don't you go up and lie down, and I'll bring you some TUMS."

"Mom, I…" I took a deep breath. "I need to talk to you."

She smiled faintly, distracted. "Of course. I'll be up in a minute, and we'll talk then."

I thought of Edgar in the closet, listening to our conversation. My stomach lurched. Maybe I really *was* sick.

"Can we talk here? It's important."

Mom pulled up a chair at the kitchen table. "Of course. What's this about, Josh?"

"Well…" I checked the front window, making sure Michael wasn't strolling up the walk. "It's Michael. He keeps going in my room."

I knew those words would get her attention. My mom was a firm believer in a person's right to privacy, even if that person was a kid. As long as I made sure my room wasn't a disaster, Mom had promised she would never go through my stuff. She was pretty cool that way.

"Are you sure?"

"Yeah."

"How can you tell?"

I told her about Edgar, and how I kept hiding him in the closet, only to find him on my pillow. Mom sighed as I spoke, shaking her head slightly. Once I was quiet again, she reached across the table for my hand and gave it a little squeeze.

"Josh, I know this has been tough on you. It's been a big adjustment for both of us, having Michael move in. But it's been hard on Michael too—he just wants to be your friend. I don't like that he's been going through your things, and I'll speak to him about that, but can't you keep the bear on your bed? It means so much to him, and I'm sure you don't really care one way or another."

The last thing I wanted to do was let her down, but this was my one chance to tell her how I felt without Michael looming over us with his sharky smile. "I really don't like it, Mom. It creeps me out. I can't sleep with it—it'll give me nightmares. Can you get Michael to take it back?"

She studied my face. Often it seemed like she could read my mind, but not today. "Can't you give him a chance? He's trying."

"This isn't about Michael, Mom—it isn't, I promise. It's just the bear. I really don't like the bear. Will you *please* ask him if he'll take it back?"

A strange expression clouded her features, and she too glanced out the window to make sure the coast was clear. That was the trouble with funerals—you never knew how long they were going to last. At any moment, Michael could be home again.

I was surprised to see that she seemed nervous. What was she afraid of? Michael was her husband. She loved him…didn't she?

"To be honest," she said, lowering her voice even though we were the only people in the house, "I don't like that bear, either. It looks… *evil*."

I gaped at her in shock. My mother was a religious, God-fearing woman. She didn't use the word *evil* lightly. In fact, I didn't think I'd ever heard her say it before.

She studied me for another moment and then made up her mind. "Okay, I'll ask him to take it back. I'm not sure what I'm going to say, but I'll think of something that won't hurt his feelings too much." Her brow wrinkled in concern. "You don't look well. You should rest. Will you be okay with the bear for now, or do you want me to take it until Michael gets home?"

A ripple of fear coursed through my body. It was so strong that it nearly knocked me to my knees. "No, don't take it!" I yelled. It was something about the bear, about Edgar and my mother. As crazy as it was, I knew I had to protect her from Edgar. I could never leave her alone with that thing.

Mom took a step back at my reaction and her face went pale, but she recovered quickly. "All right, then, we'll leave it where it is. You go lie down now, and I'll bring you those TUMS."

I thought of Edgar and his sinister grin, Edgar's yellow eyes glowing in the darkness of my closet, and shivered. And what if it was worse? What if the bear was on my bed again? Michael wasn't here to pin the blame on this time. If I walked into my room and saw Edgar on my bed, I'd die.

"Can I stay in the living room?"

It may have been my imagination, but I swear Mom was relieved. "I think that's a good idea," she said.

By the time Michael got home, I was feeling much better. Mom had placed a cold cloth on my forehead and let me drink all the ginger ale I wanted. She'd put on my favorite cartoons too. As long as I didn't have to be alone with the bear, I was happy.

When I heard the back door open, I put down my glass and laid my head on the cushions. I could hear Mom talking to Michael in low tones out in the kitchen, and I knew exactly what they were talking about—Edgar. Closing my eyes, I pretended to be asleep. I stayed that way until they were done talking, even when I heard Michael come into the room and walk up to the couch.

I could hear him breathing. His eyes were burning a hole in my face. I could feel him watching me for a minute, or five, ten—maybe twenty years. Finally I couldn't stand it any longer, and I let my eyes flutter open, trying to make it seem like I had just woken up.

Michael's features were twisted into an expression of hatred so ugly that I gasped. I knew then that he wasn't trying to be my friend—that he didn't and had never liked me. At that moment, I wasn't sure if he liked my mother.

When he saw I was awake, that terrible sneer vanished so quickly that I wondered if I'd seen it at all. It was replaced by his usual bland expression. "I understand you've been having some problems with Edgar," he said in that cheerful way of his, but it gave me the creeps. Why did he insist on talking about that bear as if it were a person?

He leaned close to me then, so close I could smell the sourness of cigars on his breath. Michael often enjoyed a smoke with his grieving clients. Mom didn't approve, but what could she do? Michael insisted the smoking was important for his business.

"I *told* you not to put him in the closet," he said. "Edgar likes to sleep in a proper bed."

I inched away from him, squeezing myself as far into the cushions as I could, trying to put some distance between his stale cigar breath and me.

"You shouldn't have gone through my closet," I said, hoping I didn't sound as scared as I felt. "My room is private."

He smirked. "I think we both know I didn't go in your closet. You *do* know that, don't you, Josh?"

Just as I was about to put my hands over my ears and scream, my mother appeared. "Is anything wrong?"

Michael straightened, giving her one of his big phony smiles. "Of course not. Josh was just telling me he's feeling much better. Isn't that right, Josh?"

I nodded, feeling trapped but not knowing what else to do.

"Well, that's wonderful. Josh, Michael would like Edgar back. Do you think you could go get him?"

Even my phys-ed teacher had never seen me move so fast. My heart was pounding when I got to the end of the hallway, but when I opened the door, no horrible face stared back at me. Edgar had stayed where I'd left him.

I used the T-shirt trick again, wrapping the cotton fabric as if it were a shroud. Holding the bundle out in front of me, I hurried back down the hall, comforted to see that my mother was waiting in the living room with Michael. I felt safer with her there. Michael would never do anything crazy or scary as long as she was a witness.

Thrusting the wrapped bundle at him, I felt an incredible sense of relief when my stepfather's hands reached for it and lifted it out of my grasp.

Michael gently unwrapped the bear's face and cradled the teddy in his arms. My stepfather suddenly looked like the world's biggest toddler.

As soon as Mom left the room, the sneer returned to my stepfather's face. "Edgar only wanted to be your friend, but now you've gone and made him angry."

The bear seemed to tilt in his arms so Edgar's luminous yellow eyes could remain focused on me. "You really shouldn't have done that," Michael said. "When Edgar gets mad, he always gets even."

Chapter Four

I didn't sleep well that night. I dreamed of a bear with a snarling face and glowing yellow eyes. It lunged for me, its claws real and lethal amid the fuzzy fake fur of its paws. In my nightmare, it didn't matter how fast I ran. It caught me again and again, latching onto my throat and killing me.

I'd push the unsettling images out of my head, only to have them start again. The nightmare always began the same way, with the bear whispering my name.

"Josh...Josh...Jaaawwwwossssh..."

My eyes flew open. My forehead was slick with sweat, and I was panting like a trapped animal. I pulled the covers up to my nose for protection, my eyes darting this way and that, desperately trying to see in the dark.

It was just a nightmare, and I'd had many of those since Dad died. I was too curious for my own good—whenever Mom said a movie was too scary or a book too violent, I was driven to seek it out.

Nightmares were only bad dreams—they couldn't hurt me. There was no such thing as monsters, or teddy bears that came alive and grew fangs and claws. But *something* had woken me up. I waited, barely daring to breathe, my heart pounding loud enough to be heard in the next room.

I was almost asleep when I heard it again. A faint whisper, nearly drowned out by the hum of the furnace.

"Josh…"

Whimpering, I flung the covers over my head and stayed that way until morning, too terrified to cry out.

I must have drifted off, because I awakened to my mother calling my name. She sounded furious.

"Josh Leary, you get down here *right now!*"

The tone of her voice made me flinch. Sometimes Mom got frustrated with me, but I couldn't remember the last time she'd so much as raised her voice. We'd been careful with each other since we'd lost Dad.

"Josh!"

"Okay, I'm coming," I called, pulling back the covers with reluctance. My room was as it had been the day before. Nothing was out of place, at least as far as I could tell. Maybe I'd dreamed all the strange noises in the night. Or maybe Michael had been playing another one of his tricks.

I shoved my feet into my slippers and headed downstairs. Mom was in the kitchen—I could hear her voice, accompanied by the low rumble of Michael's.

Unprepared for what I was about to see, I froze in the doorway. A weird noise escaped me before I could stop it, a cross between a gasp and a shriek. The kitchen was a war zone. Mom stood in the middle of an entire week's worth of groceries. Egg yolks and ketchup streaked the floor, dotted by piles of sugar and squished fruits and vegetables. Glass jars that had once held strawberry jam and horseradish had been smashed to bits.

Mom looked like she didn't know whether to burst into tears or pull her hair out. The wildness in her eyes scared me. Michael was sitting in his usual chair at the kitchen table, smirking.

"W-what happened?" I asked.

"How could you do this?" she screamed. Flour and what appeared to be chocolate syrup streaked her face and arms. It would have been funny if I hadn't been so scared. "What were you thinking? This is hundreds of dollars' worth of food, Josh! We can't afford this."

I cringed back against the wall, frightened of my mother for the first time I could remember. "I didn't do it." Even as I said the words, I knew she wasn't going to believe me.

"Well, if you didn't, I'd sure like to know who did."

Instinctively, my eyes flicked to Michael, and that wiped the smirk off his face in a hurry. He got up from his chair, his face reddening. "I hope you're not going to try to blame this on *me*, young man."

"I-I'm not blaming anyone. I don't know what happened."

Mom was near collapse. When she'd been full of rage, it had given her energy, but now that she'd said her piece, she sagged like a deflating balloon.

"It's pretty easy to see what happened. You've been trying to cause trouble ever since I moved in," Michael said. "I realize I can't replace your father, and I'm not trying to, but you have to accept me as the man of the house, got it? This type of behavior is not going to be tolerated—not by me, and not by your mother."

I felt my eyes widen. What was he talking about? I hadn't done anything to cause trouble. "But I didn't do this!"

Michael started to respond, but my mom held up her hand, cutting him off. It seemed to take all the energy she had left. "All right, let's not fight. Josh has never lied to me, Michael. If he says he didn't do it, I believe him."

Her new husband shot her a look of disbelief, and I can't say I blamed him. Gratitude for my mother's loyalty made me feel weak in the knees, and I was glad I was still leaning against the wall.

"You must be joking, Eileen. Who else could possibly have done this? I certainly hope you don't think I'd waste my own money this way."

"I don't know who did it, and I don't want to think about it anymore. All I want is for my kitchen to be put back the way it was."

Grabbing a rag from the sink, she filled a bucket with hot soapy water. Even I could see that it was going to take a lot more than a bucket of water and soap to clean up the mess.

"Are you going to stand there all day?" Michael snapped at me. "Go help your mother."

Reluctant to cross his path, I shuffled over to where Mom kneeled on the floor, keeping my back to the wall for as long as I could. As I drew closer to her, I could see her shoulders were shaking. I wanted to hug her, but I didn't dare in front of Michael. Instead I pulled up the garbage can and started to toss in the bigger pieces of glass and eggshell.

"I have some rubber gloves under the sink. Put them on. I don't want you to cut yourself."

She still didn't meet my eyes, and I could feel the weight of her disappointment. I knew then that in spite of how she'd stuck up for me with Michael, she still thought I'd done this. As the only kid in the house, I was the most likely culprit.

When I walked to the sink, I spotted something that made me shiver. In one of the piles of sugar was a small paw print.

Chapter Five

It got so I was afraid to close my eyes. Every single night, something awful happened. It would start with that eerie whispering.

"Josh...Josh...Jaaawwwosssh..."

I began to wish that it *was* Michael playing a trick on me, but it didn't sound like Michael. There was a harshness to the whisper, something inhuman about it.

Pulling the covers over my head, I would wait, trembling, hoping whatever it was wouldn't touch me. After a while, it would get bored and I'd hear the soft pad of tiny footsteps, followed by the sound of breaking glass. I flinched at every crash, wondering why my mother never woke up. No one seemed to hear the noise but me, but they sure were able to see the destruction in the morning.

Windows were smashed. More food was smeared on the kitchen floor. And even worse, whatever it was had an unerring sense of what was most important to my mother. It destroyed her few precious things, breaking her down a little more each time. It hurt my heart to watch her cry. She begged me to tell her why I was doing such awful things. Was I angry with her? Had she done something to bring this upon herself? I would insist it hadn't been me, that I would never do that to her. Just when she believed me, Michael would interrupt, sending me to my room without breakfast so they could decide on my punishment.

When it came to punishment, Michael was becoming more and more creative. Withholding food and toys was the standard, of course, as was grounding me and not allowing me to talk to Sean or any of my other friends. But one time he made me sit in a tub of water so cold that I thought I was going to die. It hurt a lot, and tears streamed down my face as I cried and cried for my mother. I couldn't believe she would let anyone do this to me, and it was clear she wasn't happy about Michael's punishments.

"Please let him get out. That's enough," she said after I'd been in the icy water for ten minutes.

"The boy needs a firm hand, Eileen. You're not helping him by being soft. You've already let him get away with far too much."

Then he would force her out of the room and lock the door. I could hear her crying all the way down the hallway. At first I yelled for her, but Michael hit me across the face, splitting my lip. I stared at him, sucking on my wound and swallowing my own blood. It tasted like pennies, and I gagged.

"You know!" I cried. "You know it isn't me who's doing this."

"Don't be silly, Josh," he said, adding more ice cubes to the bath. "Who else could it possibly be?"

And then he slowly closed one eye and *winked* at me.

I knew then, without a doubt, that Michael was a monster.

Unfortunately for me, he decided the cold-water torture had the best chance of "straightening me out," and he kept me in the bath longer and longer. My teeth chattered. My fingers and toes and even my nails turned blue. It was extremely painful, like a million tiny knives stabbing me all over my body, but eventually I went numb and drifted away. I imagined I saw Dad during those times. He was dressed in his one good suit, and he was surrounded by light. He held open his arms when he saw me, and his cheek was wet with tears when he pressed it against mine.

"Hang on, son. You'll be all right. Just be strong for a little bit longer, okay?"

I flung my arms around him and held on so tight I would have sworn no one could make me let go, but Michael was getting better at forcing me to come back. He would pinch me under the armpits, where the skin is really tender, and once he hit me in the balls with the shampoo bottle. That made me throw up in the water, which disgusted him enough to let me go. I crawled from the tub, hands cupping my throbbing crotch, and collapsed on the bathmat, sobbing.

One time he pushed my head under so I came back choking. The water distorted his face, but I could tell he was still grinning, grinning, grinning. I don't think he would have let me up that time if Mom hadn't pounded on the door.

He knew that something was taking me away from him and the torture, that something was comforting me, and he didn't like it one bit. It made him furious. I wished he would go too far one day, and then I'd be with my dad forever. But Dad had made me promise to hold on, and so I did. I wondered what would happen if I were gone and Michael focused his cruelty on my mother.

Sometimes, in the rare moments when we were alone, Mom would hold out her arms for me. She would rest her cheek against my head and cry for ages, asking me to forgive her. I soaked up those little drops of love as if they were food for a starving man. Gone was the independent boy I'd once been, the one who'd felt he was too old for such motherly affection. Now I'd take what I could get.

Other days, she'd sit in her wicker chair in the corner, staring into space, some bit of mending or crocheting lying forgotten in her lap. It was more and more difficult to rouse her from that state, and as I shook her by the shoulders, I realized how thin and light she was. We were changing together, our cheekbones growing sharp against our skin, our eyes hollow and surrounded by shadows.

The more we wasted away, the happier Michael seemed. In spite of his diet, he was rotund as always, the swell of his stomach pressing against his proper white shirt. He was all smiles as he sat down to dinner each evening, while me and Mom (if I was allowed to eat that night) only picked at our food and said nothing.

My teachers soon noticed that something was very different about me. When I fell asleep in class for the third time in as many days, Mrs. Brinklemeir took me aside. I'd expected her to be angry with me, maybe even to hit me. Some part of me knew that teachers weren't allowed to hit their students, but such punishment had become second nature to me, to the point that I was beginning to expect it.

"Is there anything you want to tell me?" Mrs. Brinklemeir asked, her lovely face filled with concern.

Overcome with emotion, I could only shake my head. I didn't trust myself to speak.

"What's keeping you from sleeping at home? You can talk to me. You're safe here."

That was the moment I realized my beloved teacher, who I'd always thought was so smart, didn't know anything at all. School wasn't safe—*no place* was safe. If I told her what was happening at home, she'd call the police. And the police would go to Michael and tell him everything I'd said. Michael would lie. He'd tell them I'd gotten out of control, that I was acting out each night by breaking my mother's most prized possessions. He was trying to teach me a lesson, he'd say. He was trying to take a firm hand. The police would listen to him, and then they'd talk to my mother. She would back up Michael's story, because that's what she had to do. It was her way of surviving the nightmare our lives had become. And the police would believe her, if they didn't believe her husband, and they'd leave. There might be something—the suggestion of an inappropriate smirk, perhaps, or the sad condition of my mother, who had begun to resemble a prisoner of war—that would make them pause on their way out. Maybe they'd glance at each other with uncertainty, suspecting there was more to the story, but unsure of what it was. Even so, this vague niggling feeling might keep them awake that night, and for several nights to come, but it wouldn't be enough to get them to remove me from that awful house, to take me someplace safe. Or better yet, to lock Michael away somewhere so we'd never have to see him again.

The police would leave, and I'd be left with a man even angrier than before. So no, there was no place safe. Not for me, at least.

A few days after Mrs. Brinklemeir pulled me aside, something happened that changed everything. Whatever was responsible for the destruction in our house finally went too far.

It went after my mother's cookie jar.

The jar was very old. It had been my great-grandmother's, and Mom had told me that she thought it must have been made in the 1930s, maybe even the '20s. But it wasn't its age that made it special—it was the memories it contained.

Mom had spent her childhood summers on her grandmother's farm. As a young girl, she had been fascinated with the jar, which was decorated with the most amazing painted cookies. She used to stare at them for hours, imagining what those cookies would taste like if they were inside the jar instead of her grandmother's usual oatmeal raisin or chocolate chip. And I completely understood, because I used to do the same thing. When it came time to get a real cookie, though, Mom insisted on being the one who retrieved it from the jar. Time had made the ceramic brittle, and she worried that I would break it, destroying her childhood memories in one fell swoop.

That morning, I was woken up by a strange noise. As I strained to hear what had awakened me, it happened again. It was the sound of hysterical sobbing.

I leapt out of bed and tore from the room, taking the stairs to the main floor two at a time. "Mom! Mom, are you okay?"

I stopped short when I got to the kitchen. Mom was cradling a broken bit of pottery to her chest. She was wailing.

I wanted to go to her, but Michael blocked my path. "I hope you're happy now. I hope you got what you wanted, because you are going to be punished within an inch of your life."

At his words, my mother stopped crying. Her head shot up and her eyes narrowed as she glared at him. "No! Enough is enough. You leave him alone."

The shocked expression on his face was the best thing I'd seen in a long time.

"You're still going to protect him? You've got to be joking, Eileen. He destroyed the thing you love most in the world." Underneath his words lurked that threat I'd heard so much of lately. My mother didn't flinch.

"The thing I love most is my *son*, Michael. I was wrong to let you discipline him. You're not his father, and I think your punishments have driven a bigger wedge between you."

A bigger wedge? If Michael and I stood on either side of the Grand Canyon, we couldn't be farther apart.

Michael's face turned red, then purple. His skin got so dark I thought his head would explode. He stood there, unclenching and clenching his fists. "Fine," he said, spitting each word from between gritted teeth. "Have it your way, but you deserve everything you get. I'm going out."

He stormed out of the kitchen and was gone in a matter of minutes, slamming the door. For once Mom didn't run after him. She wept, letting the broken piece of porcelain slip from her fingers. I crept over to her, unsure of her reaction. I didn't think she would slap me, but who knew? I was so used to being the scapegoat that I jumped if a car backfired.

When I was close enough to touch, she hugged me with a ferocity that nearly knocked me off my feet. I pressed my cheek against her shoulder and she leaned her head against mine. We stayed like that for a long time.

"I've gotten us into quite a mess, haven't I?" Her eyes were unbearably sad.

"I didn't do it, Mom. You have to believe me! I would never break your cookie jar."

I thought I saw a faint glimmer of hope flicker in her eyes. "I didn't think so," she said, her words slow and careful. "I didn't think you would do a thing like that." She seized me by the shoulders suddenly, startling me so I gasped. "But who did, Josh? Who is doing this? Please tell me."

I felt the sensation of something sneaking up behind me, creeping closer and closer on silent feet. The urge to look over my shoulder was overwhelming, but equally strong was the instinct that told me it was better not to know. "Is Michael back?" I whispered.

She frowned, but shook her head. "No, we're alone. Please tell me. Who is doing this?"

Squeezing my eyes shut, I told her the truth. "Edgar."

Mom wrapped her arms around me and held me for a long time. She didn't say another word. Eventually she sent me off to play while she cleaned up the broken china. Michael came home later that night with reddened eyes, smelling of beer. He went to bed without speaking to either of us.

The next day, Mom told me I was going to see a doctor.

Chapter Six

"Your mother tells me there's been some problems at home."

Dr. Harvey seemed nice. He was a little old man with lots of white hair and a little white goatee. He wore a pale blue sweater and smelled of mint. I'd bet he was someone's grandpa.

"Are you going to give me a needle?"

He laughed, but it was in a kind way, not in that mean kids-say-the-stupidest-things way some adults have. "Nope, no needles, and I won't listen to your heart, either. I'm not that type of doctor, Josh."

I narrowed my eyes. "Then what type of doctor are you?" I couldn't understand why I had to spend a Saturday in Dr. Harvey's office, as nice as he was. I wasn't sick. And no doctor in the world would be able to stop Edgar.

"I'm more interested with what's going on in here," he said, tapping the side of his head. "I want to know what you're thinking, what you're feeling."

"Why?"

"Your mother thinks you might need someone to talk to. Do *you* think you need someone to talk to?"

"No," I said. I leaned back against the chair and crossed my arms. *This is stupid.*

"What do you think of your stepfather?"

I kicked my feet, thunking my heels against the chair. It made a satisfying sound. *Tha-thunk. Tha-thunk. Tha-thunk.* I silently dared Dr. Harvey to tell me to stop, but he didn't notice. He was still waiting for me to answer. I shrugged. "He's okay." *For a monster.*

"Is he? Your mother thinks you don't like him very much."

I shrugged again. Dr. Harvey leaned toward me, gripping the arms of my chair. I had to stop kicking if I didn't want to hurt him, so I did. "Josh, there's something I need you to know. Anything you tell me is confidential. Do you know what that means?"

"Yep. You won't tell anyone."

"That's right. I'm your doctor, and I'd like to be your friend. You can tell me anything you like, and I won't repeat it to a single soul."

"But I don't need a doctor. I'm not sick."

Dr. Harvey smiled. "Of course you're not sick. You seem to me to be a very healthy young man. People come to see me when something is bothering them. Maybe they're having bad thoughts, or they have nightmares all the time. Maybe someone is picking on them, or being mean to them."

A tiny spark of interest was growing in my mind. "Do you help those people?" I asked. Behind his wire-rimmed glasses, Dr. Harvey's eyes were blue and very kind. I could tell he was a man who smiled a lot.

"I'd like to think so. Sometimes it helps people to talk to someone who they can trust. And you can trust me. I'm on your side."

"And you won't tell Michael anything I say?"

He made a zipping motion across his lips. "Not a word."

I thought for a moment. I was old enough to know that the things Michael had been doing to me were very, very wrong. If anyone found out, he would be in a lot of trouble, maybe even go to jail. And then what would happen to Mom? Would she hate me? Would we lose our house and have to live on the street? Maybe I'd have to quit school and get a job. But who would hire a ten-year-old kid?

Dr. Harvey continued to study me, waiting. I squirmed in the seat, wishing I were invisible. What if I told the truth and Michael found out somehow? What if they didn't do anything to him, and he was still in the house with Mom and me? What if he tried to really hurt me?

"Are you afraid of your stepfather, Josh?"

After a minute, I nodded. Nodding wasn't really *saying* anything, after all. I couldn't get in trouble for nodding.

"Can you tell me what he does that frightens you?"

More uncomfortable minutes passed. I could feel Dr. Harvey's eyes on me as he waited for me to say something. He seemed to be willing to wait for as long as it took.

"Remember, Josh—you can tell me anything, and Michael will never find out. I won't even tell your mother. I promise."

"I think he hates me," I mumbled, staring at my hands. There was something about Dr. Harvey that made me scared to meet his eyes. What if he could tell what I was thinking?

"Why do you think that?" Dr. Harvey asked. He was the first adult who didn't insist on arguing with me. I didn't want to hear that Michael didn't hate me, because I knew he did.

He *had* to hate me to give me that bear.

I said nothing. Dr. Harvey was leaning back in his own chair now, so I resumed kicking. *Tha-thunk. Tha-thunk. Tha-thunk.*

"Does he say mean things to you?"

I nodded.

"Does he ever hit you?"

"Not really," I whispered. If I told the truth, he'd report it, and then Michael would know what I'd done.

"Josh, does Michael…does he ever touch you in an inappropriate way?"

My eyes widened, but Dr. Harvey wasn't disgusted or angry; he looked just as he had when he'd asked me the other questions. My stomach churned—I knew exactly what he was getting at, and the very thought made me sick. "No, never."

The doctor wrote something down on his clipboard. "How long has Michael been saying mean things to you?"

"Since he gave me Edgar."

The thought of the bear and its twisted snout and evil yellow eyes made me feel cold.

"And Edgar is the teddy bear, correct?"

I nodded.

"Josh, why do you think Michael gave you Edgar?"

"Because he hates me," I said.

Chapter Seven

Meeting Dr. Harvey was one of the best things that could have happened to me. Just knowing that there was someone I could talk to every week who would listen gave me courage.

The one thing I could not talk about was Edgar. Every week, Dr. Harvey asked about him, and every week I managed to change the subject. Telling my mom the truth was one thing, but I knew I could never tell another adult. Not unless I wanted to be hauled off to the place where crazy people go.

The bolder I got, the weaker Michael became. Ever since I started seeing Dr. Harvey, Michael didn't hit me anymore. The ice-water baths stopped. He rarely raised his voice. Instead, he simply avoided me. It was an uneasy peace, but much better than how things had been before.

The destruction stopped too. I know Mom suspected that talking to Dr. Harvey was letting me express my anger in a healthy way. It hurt that she didn't believe me, but maybe it was better. I was a kid and *I* could barely handle it. The truth would probably be enough to drive Mom crazy.

As for Edgar, I hardly saw him anymore. Sometimes I thought I caught a glimpse of him out of the corner of my eye, and other times I was awakened by something painful but half-remembered, only to find a strange bruise on my cheek or a red mark on my arm. After a while, even that stopped happening. I thought I'd finally seen the last of Edgar.

Sadly, I was wrong.

About a month after I started seeing Dr. Harvey, it happened again. Someone whispering my name startled me out of a deep sleep.

"Josh...Josh...Jaaawwwwosssh..."

This time, instead of cowering under the covers and praying for morning to come, I snapped on the light. Wincing at the sudden brightness, I looked around the room, darting quick glances at every shadowy corner.

Nothing.

I was alone.

"Who's there?" I demanded, knowing once and for all that the whisperer wasn't Michael. There was no way he would have been able to find a place to hide so quickly.

Crossing my arms, I prepared to wait. Within a few short minutes, I heard it again.

"Josh...Josh...Jaaawwwwosssh..."

I leapt out of bed. "Where are you?" I yelled, not caring who I woke up. Seizing my Yoda flashlight, I shined it under the bed. I searched in my closet and in my toy chest. Nothing.

By the time I climbed back into bed, my pajama top was sticking to my sweat-soaked skin. I was determined to stay up the rest of the night, to catch Edgar in the act and to prove once and for all, even to myself, that he was the one who tormented me.

But the excitement of the search had gotten to me, and soon enough, my eyes closed. I fell asleep with the lights on, my Yoda flashlight clutched in one hand.

I was standing in a field. The sun beat warm against my face, and

I could smell the rich soil and the faint perfume of wildflowers. A man headed toward me from across the field—slower at first, and then faster and faster. I wasn't surprised to see the man was my father, because I knew I was dreaming. He was much the same, except there were streaks of silver in his blond hair, and more smile lines around his eyes.

He held out his arms for me, and I ran to embrace him.

"Dad!"

I buried my face in his shoulder, breathing in the familiar scent of his cologne. I never wanted to let him go, but all too soon Dad pulled back from me. Rather than being thrilled to see me, he looked worried. "Your mother is in trouble, Josh."

"What? Why?"

"You have to save her."

Mom, in trouble? I knew she hadn't been happy lately, but it wasn't as if she was the one who had her head pushed under water.

"What's wrong with Mom?"

"It's the bear. You have to get rid of the bear, Josh. You have to get rid of Edgar."

At the mention of his name, it was as if the sun went behind a cloud. "But how? I don't even know where he is anymore."

"He's never far from you. All you have to do is keep your eyes open, and you'll see him. You must destroy him."

A sharp, stabbing pain in my foot made me cry out. My father reached out a hand to steady me. "What is it, son? What's wrong?"

"I don't know," I said, hopping on one leg as I clutched my injured foot. "I think something bit me!"

Another shot of intense pain, this time in my other foot, made me scream. I collapsed to the ground, rocking back and forth. Lightning traveled through my nerve endings, pain so intense I could barely stand it. My dad bent to gather me in his arms.

"He knows you're with me. He can see us. Nowhere is safe right now, Josh, not even in your head. Every time you come to me you will be punished, do you understand? If you want to keep visiting me, you'll have to destroy the bear. Can you promise? Promise me you'll destroy it."

I shrieked as my left foot was the victim of another vicious bite. Curling into the fetal position, I moaned as Dad tried to comfort me.

"Go back, son," he said. "Go back, and he won't hurt you anymore."

I opened my eyes. The field of wildflowers was gone. In its place was only darkness. *Why was it so dark?* I was sure I'd left the light on. My feet still throbbed with pain, but it wasn't as bad as it had been in the dream. I pushed on the switch of my Yoda flashlight. *Click-click. Click-click.* The battery was dead. I must have fallen asleep before I could turn the flashlight off.

I reached for the lamp, but before I could touch the switch, something soft grazed my hand. I bit my lip to keep from crying out. Waiting in the dark, I held my breath, my eyes squeezed shut. I didn't want to see the yellow eyes that I knew would be staring back at me. Finally I got up the nerve to fumble for the lamp again. This time nothing touched me.

Slowly, I risked a peek. My room was empty again. I was alone.

But embedded in my feet were three brass tacks.

Chapter Eight

Sean sounded surprised to hear from me that weekend. I guess I couldn't blame him; we hadn't really spoken in weeks. Either I was grounded or I was too ashamed over the latest punishment to want to see anyone.

"What do you want to do?" he asked as we sat in my backyard, popping the heads off the dandelions. It was Saturday afternoon, a sunny June day that held a promise of the summer to come. I was determined Edgar would be out of our lives before school was out. There was no way I could handle being in the house with him all week.

"Let's go treasure hunting." The weather had definitely worked in my favor. If it had been raining, Sean would never have agreed to my plan.

"Asstastic! Where do you want to go? The train tracks?" There was always plenty of treasure to be found at the rail yards. We both had an impressive collection of rusty iron spikes.

"Nah, let's go to the dump. Do you know how to get there?"

Sean's eyes widened. The town dump was a half-day ride on our bikes, easy. It also required sneaking past Mr. McGilvery, who stood guard at the huge gate and charged people money for the privilege of getting rid of their old junk. Scavenging in the dump was strictly forbidden. We both knew kids who had done it successfully, but we also knew more kids who had gotten caught.

"Sure, I guess I do, but that's pretty far. What about the lake?" The lake was about ten blocks from my house. Some people liked to sit on the small bit of sand that surrounded it and pretend it was a beach. As a result, it was a good place to find treasure too—lost earrings, bits of change, keys. Sean had found a dirty magazine there once, and was always hoping that lightning would strike twice.

"Nah, we went there last time. Besides, I wanna drop something off."

Sean's eyes gleamed. The guy was a walking radar detector when it came to mischief. "Whatcha got, Josh?"

I shrugged, being careful to stay casual. If I gave Sean any reason to suspect how scared I was, one of two things would happen—he'd get freaked out and refuse to go, or he'd tease me so bad I'd never hear the end of it. Neither were great options. "Just that ugly bear of my stepfather's. I want to get rid of it."

I needn't have worried. Sean threw his head back and laughed, a long, high cackle. "Asstastic! We'll be pirates, and the ugly-ass bear can be our prisoner."

I liked the thought of Edgar being at our mercy. I was glad Sean had agreed, because one thing was for sure—I wouldn't have had the guts to go without him.

Finding Edgar had been a challenge. Once I made sure my mom was working in her garden, I crept into her bedroom. Since Michael had moved in, they'd been keeping it locked, but I could open it easily with my plastic library card. My pulse pounding in my throat, I hurriedly searched their closet and dresser drawers. I even looked under their bed, cold sweat running along the tip of my nose. But I didn't find anything, much less that dreaded teddy bear. I wondered why Michael was so determined to keep me out of his room. He certainly didn't have anything worth hiding.

Where was that damn bear?

I remembered my dad's words from last night's dream. My hands were trembling as I left Mom's room, careful to lock the door behind me. With a sinking heart, I tiptoed into my own room, cursing myself for being silly. What was I trying to sneak up on?

I didn't bother to answer my own unspoken question. I knew *exactly* why I was being sneaky.

Edgar was in the first place I looked, lying in my closet underneath the pile of clothes. I was expecting to see him, but I still had to bite my lip to keep from yelling when I saw him in the gloom, leering up at me.

Before I could lose my nerve, I threw an old blanket over the bear and wrapped him in it as tightly as I could, tying the bundle with an old skipping rope. Then I stuffed Edgar, blanket and all, into my backpack. I hadn't had the guts to put the backpack on yet, and as Sean and I talked, I kept glancing over at it, expecting to see it move.

"Well, what are you waiting for? Let's go!" Sean was practically hopping from foot to foot with excitement. I knew it was going to be hard to keep up with him. On a normal day, he was a faster rider than I was, but with an adventure ahead, he'd take off like a rocket.

"Just a minute," I said. "I need to tell my mom we're going."

Mom was bent over her flowerbed. With a sad little pang, I saw there were strands of gray in her light brown hair. Just like Dad in Heaven or wherever he was, she was getting older.

I had to call her name a few times before she answered. She looked around with a puzzled expression, almost as if she didn't know where she was. Purple shadows circled her eyes, so dark they were like bruises.

"Did you call me, Josh?"

"Yeah. Sean and I are going to go on a treasure hunt. Is that okay?"

She squinted up at me, using one gloved hand to shield her eyes from the sun. "I guess so. Are you going to the lake?"

Crap. I hadn't expected her to ask me where we were going. Usually she only needed to know what I was doing and with whom. "Yeah, and a couple other places." I felt heavy with the guilt of lying to her.

"You'll be back before dinner?"

"Well, here's the thing. Sean's mom is ordering pizza, and she asked me if I could go over there for dinner. Is that okay?"

Mom's face relaxed. She appeared relieved that I'd be someone else's problem that evening, and I knew what she was thinking—the less time Michael and I spent in each other's company, the better.

"I don't see why not. It's good to see you spending time with your friends again."

"Yeah. Hey, Mom, can I borrow one of those shovel things?"

She was confused until she saw that I was pointing to the garden tool she held. "You mean a spade? Why on earth would you need a spade?"

I rolled my eyes, trying to seem as exasperated as possible. "Geez, Mom! How are we supposed to dig for buried treasure if we don't have a shovel?"

Mom smiled, the first real smile I'd seen from her in a while. It didn't erase the sadness in her eyes, but at least it was a start. "Of course. I should have realized." She handed me the tool, its business end already coated in dirt. "You better wash that off first, or you'll get your things all mucky."

I agreed, but I had no intention of cleaning it. Let Edgar get a bit dirty—it would serve him right.

That bike ride was the strangest of my life, and I hope never to repeat it. Sean grinned when he heard my story of the pizza supper at his house.

"That's perfect! That will give us the time we need to get there and back." He threw his leg over his bike and sighed. "I kinda wish we *were* going to the lake and eating pizza at my house. It would be a lot easier."

"You don't have to come if you don't want to," I said, knowing full well that Sean wouldn't be able to resist the challenge. "I can go by myself."

As we soon learned, Sean was right to have reservations. We hadn't been pedaling for more than twenty minutes before thick, dark storm clouds clustered above us.

"Well, I'll be a monkey's vagina! Where in the ever lovin' crap did those come from? It's supposed to be sunny all day."

Before I could answer, lightning flashed from one cloud to the next, bright enough to blind us. I swerved, nearly hitting a rock and toppling my bike. I had an unsettling feeling, but I kept pedaling as fast as I could. "Come on! If we hurry, we can make it there before it rains."

Sean grumbled, but he was soon hard on my heels. The chrome of our spokes flashed with every lightning strike. When the thunder came, it was powerful enough to make the ground vibrate under our wheels. I wobbled again, the original uneasy rider.

"Holy kumquat sheeeit!" Sean cried, fighting to keep his balance. And then the rain came.

I'd been caught in the rain before. Sometimes I'd intentionally sought it out. But never before had I felt anything like this. Every droplet of water was a tiny knife, stabbing at any inch of bare skin. We bent our heads over our handlebars and worked the pedals like we were in the Tour de France, crying out as the rain struck a particularly vulnerable part. It was like getting slapped a million times, or stung by an army of tiny hornets.

"Is this all you got, Edgar?" I spat the words from between gritted teeth, confident Sean couldn't hear me over the storm. "A little rain isn't going to stop us."

We were able to take the trail along McGiver's Forest most of the way. The trees offered us some protection from the storm, but eventually we ran out of options. It was either the street or the sidewalk. We paused, surveying the crosswalk that ran across Seventh Avenue, one of the busiest streets in town. Seen through the sheet of rain, the lights of the cars were blurred smears of red and gold.

"Should we cross?" Sean asked. The other side of the avenue was more sheltered, but I shook my head. I had a vision of a car trying to stop in time, but unable to, its tires shrieking on the wet pavement, the horrified face of the driver right before he hit us...

"Let's stay on this side."

We lowered our heads again and pushed off, the rain striking our necks and backs and legs. Our clothing was soaked, but it made me feel better to think that Edgar was probably soaked too, as my backpack wasn't waterproof. *Let him drown in there,* I thought, and as I did, I felt my pack jostle against my back. I panicked, nearly losing my balance. My hands tightened on the handlebars.

It's only your imagination.

But I knew it hadn't been.

We'd gotten out of the forest just in time. There was a loud cracking noise, and another blinding flash behind us. We both skidded to a stop and turned to watch.

"Holy assbat Jesus." Sean whistled. "Did you see that?"

I was too stunned to reply. Lightning was hitting the trees. One by one they caught fire and fell. Soon a steady stream of chipmunks, squirrels, and birds was fleeing the forest. We even saw a deer run past.

The lightning continued to flash, every strike a direct hit. With each crackle and hiss, we both jumped. Our shoulders were so hunched they almost touched our ears. Sean stared at me, wincing into the rain, his eyes wide with fear. "This isn't right, man."

"Let's get out of here." I didn't need to ask him twice. Soon we were moving away from McGiver's Forest as fast as we could go, fighting for purchase on the slick sidewalk.

We hadn't gone much farther, maybe another mile or two, when we saw the worms. They covered the path ahead in thick, pink ropes. I could almost hear the squelching. One thing I'd never told Sean is that I was afraid of worms. It wasn't something a boy my age would ever admit to his buddies, unless he wanted to find a few worms in his sleeping bag on the next camping trip.

My chest tightened as I saw their disgusting, slimy bodies. They were night crawlers, the biggest of the big, and they were everywhere. My mouth went as dry as dust. I couldn't swallow.

I could hear Sean swearing up ahead. The scene was enough to gross *him* out, and as far as I knew, he wasn't afraid of worms. Apparently deciding that the best thing to do was get it over with, my friend picked up speed. Cold worm guts splashed me in the face. My stomach clenched with the need to puke, but I kept on going, focusing on my friend's broad back.

I could avoid seeing them, but I couldn't stop hearing the sickening splat they made as our tires ran over them, crushing them into the concrete. Still, we were nearly past. My spirits rose, and even the rain seemed to be letting up. We could do this! We *would* do this.

And then Sean braked so suddenly I almost crashed into him.

"Jesus Jumping Liversnaps!" he screamed. "Holy monkey ass cock knocker!"

I pulled alongside, careful not to see the ground. I didn't want to stop, because I'd have to put my feet down, so I circled in front. "What's—" I started to ask, but then I saw.

Sean's face was as white as milk. He was staring at his front tire, and his eyes were so big I was worried they would burst from his face. Curled through his spokes was a snake.

Garter snakes were pretty common in the fields nearby, and neither of us had a problem with them. We'd both kept them as pets and used them to scare girls. But garter snakes were harmless. Garter snakes didn't hiss or spit. We knew this wasn't a garter snake.

The creature reared back as if to strike, and Sean screamed. "Josh, what do I do? What do I do? It's going to bite me."

He was paralyzed with fear—otherwise he would have thrown down his bike and ran to safety, worms or no worms. I could see that if he continued sitting there, the snake was going to bite him, and maybe even kill him. So I said the only thing I could think of.

"Pedal, Sean! Pedal! It'll fall off."

I wasn't sure if it would or not, but I figured anything was better than sitting there in the rain, waiting for the snake to bite. Sean took off with a yell, moving faster than ever before, pedaling as if his life depended on it. Which I guess it did, in a way. I could barely keep up, and soon it was hard to make out his yellow bike through the rain, but I could still hear him cussing.

Then I was riding over splotches of blood and bits of snake flesh, and I knew something had cut the grotesque reptile, slicing it to ribbons. I called for Sean to slow down—I knew our speed was dangerous, especially so close to the road, but the storm stole the words from my mouth and carried them in the opposite direction.

I went another mile without seeing a glimpse of my friend. Cold fear gripped my heart, and I worked harder. I'd never forgive myself if something had happened to Sean, but suddenly there he was, straddling his bike on the sidewalk. Seeing him gave me new energy, and I picked up speed, circling in front of him once more.

His red hair was nearly black from the rain and plastered to his poor pale face. Every clash of thunder made him tremble.

"Are you all right?" I asked, aware that the pack on my back had gained weight and was growing heavier by the second. We didn't have much time. Lightning lit up the sky, making his freckles stand out in stark relief.

"I—I think so," he said, and I could see in his eyes that he was truly terrified. Guilt added to the weight on my shoulders. I'd never told my friend that Edgar was much more than your average teddy bear. He'd had no idea what we were in for, but then again, neither had I. "How much farther, do you think?"

Peering through the driving rain, I saw that we were no longer in the town center. We'd been so concerned with the storm, the worms, and the snake that we hadn't realized how far we'd come. Warehouses and factories with their bleak smokestacks rose out of the gloom.

"Not far. Maybe half an hour?" I guessed.

My heart leapt with hope. We were so close, and soon Edgar would be buried deep in the town dump, never to be seen again. The storm had been fierce enough that Mr. McGilvery was certain to have gone inside instead of waiting at his post by the gate. That would make sneaking in so much easier.

By unspoken agreement, we continued to cycle, and somehow the rain didn't bother me as much anymore. It was like that moment in a race when you first glimpse the finish line. We had the wind at our backs and nothing was going to stop us.

We were flying past the town limits, leaving the storm behind us, our spirits soaring. Even Sean seemed to understand that we had passed some terrible test. He pumped his fist in the air and yodeled, turning back to flash me one of his trademark grins.

Before I could return the gesture, I heard it. The sound of tires screeching as they turned a corner, a car's engine roaring as it chased after us. My fingers tightened on the handlebars again, and I picked up my pace, determined to close the distance between Sean and me.

I was convinced the car was behind me, so I wasn't prepared for what came next. A black sedan that was all too familiar lurched out of the grayness of the afternoon, jumped the curb, and pulled onto the sidewalk in front of Sean. I screamed to warn my friend, but the storm had stolen my voice. I braked and watched in horror as the bike and the sedan careened toward each other. Sean managed to stop just seconds short of collision.

My heart leapt into my throat hard enough to choke me. I could have sworn something shifted in my pack again. By the time I'd recovered enough to join my friend, Sean was off his bike and yelling at the car, using his best swears and the most obscene gestures he could think of. I tugged his sleeve, knowing what was to come, and hoping we could get far, far away before it happened.

It was too late.

The driver's side door popped open. My stepfather got out of the car and towered over us, glaring.

"Oh sheeeit," I heard Sean mutter under his breath.

"What are you boys doing all the way out here? This is no place for children." If he'd meant to sound concerned, he was failing horribly.

"Just going for a ride," I said, fighting to keep my voice steady. He continued to stare at me in that spooky way he had, oblivious to the beads of rain that formed on his suit lapels and the pools of water on his good shoes.

"For a ride? In Industrial Park? Does your mother know you come all the way out here? I don't think she'd approve." He took a threatening step toward me. "*I* certainly don't."

Sean hurried to get between us. "We're good cyclists, sir. And we need the practice if we're going to be allowed to participate in the big charity cycle in August."

I never failed to be amazed by my friend's smarts. The charity cycle was a long-distance bike ride that raised money for some disease or the starving kids in the Sudan or something. No kids had participated before, but there was no reason we couldn't be the first.

"That's an honorable goal, boys, but do you really think it's a good idea to be practicing in this?" Michael gestured to the sky so the rain thrummed against his palm, water running through his fingers like blood.

"We can't miss a one, sir. The charity cycle will be here before we know it." When I saw the expression on Michael's face, it was all I could do not to seize my friend by his collar and haul him safely out of striking distance.

"It's too dangerous." My stepfather took another step closer, the leather of his good shoes soaked and turning darker. "I'm sorry, boys, but I'm afraid you're going to have to turn back. It's not safe for you to be out in this. Your mothers would have my head if I let you continue."

His thick, hammy fingers tightened into fists as he waited to see what I would do. My backpack gave a huge lurch, as if Edgar was trying to claw his way out. Michael's eyes widened, but not as much as Sean's.

"What on earth do you have in that bag?" Michael asked, but I could see in his eyes that he knew *exactly* what was in my pack. I nodded at Sean—it was just the slightest tip of my chin, but my friend understood. Without another word to Michael, I bent low over my handlebars and took off as fast as I could, swerving off the sidewalk and cutting into the concrete jungle of parking lots that surrounded us.

I guided my bike around orange pylons and the huge *Road Closed* signs that were like small fences. Anytime I spotted an obstacle that would make it impossible for a car to follow us, I headed in that direction. By the time we reached the dump, Michael and his black sedan were nowhere to be seen.

The rain had quieted to a gentle drizzle as we stashed our bikes in a nearby ditch and sprinted for the hole in the chain-link fence. The torn and twisted metal reached out to restrain us, snagging our shirts and jeans and tearing a large patch from one of Sean's socks, but we pushed on, our hands and knees slick with cold mud as we slid through the opening.

As suspected, Mr. McGilvery was nowhere to be found. We stayed low to the ground as we scurried through the dump, searching for a hiding place where we could rest. Finally we found an old truck that still had a working door and climbed inside, pressing our backs gratefully against the seat, which was leaking yellow stuffing and had a funny smell. I tossed my pack outside, where it landed in the mud. Edgar didn't deserve shelter.

Sean let out a low whistle. "That was close," he said, causing us both to collapse into helpless giggles. We laughed until we were nearly sick, clutching our sides and our sore stomachs. "Your stepfather is one scary-ass monkey weasel."

I was too weak from laughing to speak. My friend was quiet for a moment while we both calmed down. "That bear…it isn't just a toy, is it?"

I shook my head. I had no proof, but I was willing to bet that everything that had happened so far was Edgar's doing, from the storm to the sudden appearance of my stepfather.

"Well, then let's get rid of the ugly mofo. I don't know about you, but I don't want to spend the rest of my weekend hanging around here."

We climbed out of the truck as quietly as we could, scanning the piles of garbage for any sign of McGilvery. Our spirits had lightened along with the storm and soon we made it into a game, acting like G.I. Joe on a mission as we crept among the piles of garbage. I was glad I was staying over at Sean's that night—there would be no explaining the unsavory mess I was making of my jeans. Not to mention how awesome it would be to have a full evening without Michael.

Sean wrinkled his nose as we passed one particularly ripe pile of trash. "Nasty."

"Let's stop here. This is perfect."

"Here?"

"Trust me, this is where Edgar belongs."

"Edgar?" My friend's eyes lit up like they always did when he saw

an opportunity to taunt someone, but he still took a step back when I unzipped my pack.

"What is it, Sean? Scared of a little teddy bear?" Snickering, I reached into the bag, only to yank my hand back with a yelp. Several drops of blood appeared at the tip of my index finger.

"W-what happened?" The color had returned to my friend's cheeks during our little landfill adventure, but now he was that sickly white again. He retreated another step.

"I-I think it *bit* me." Before Sean could burst into another round of laughter, I held up my hand. Blood from the wound trickled down my finger in a race to my wrist. There wasn't a lot of it, but it hurt like hell. My entire hand throbbed in sympathy.

"That's sincerely messed up." He looked askance at the bag as if it contained a bomb rather than a teddy bear. "What are we going to do?"

As I sucked my finger to numb the pain and stop the bleeding, I felt something unusual—*rage.* The anger started in my stomach as a hot coal, and grew and grew, until I could taste fire in my throat. I grabbed my backpack by the strap and, flipping it over, shook it as hard as I could. Mom's spade fell to the ground with a clunk, narrowly missing my toes. Edgar failed to make an appearance, but that was okay. I didn't need to see him in order to bury him.

Throwing my pack to the ground, I started to dig. My eyes watered from the stench of years and years' worth of garbage. Old diapers, rotten vegetables, cans crusted over with dried gunk that looked like boogers—I had to breathe through my mouth to keep from retching. The more frantically I swung the little shovel, the more Sean retreated, until he was standing several feet away.

"That's good enough! Toss it in, and let's get the hell out of here."

I knew he was right. I was up to my knees in trash, and the hole I'd dug was so deep that the ground underneath me was feeling soft. One wrong move and I'd slide down into the sinkhole I'd created.

Reaching into my bag for Edgar again was more than I could handle, but the thought of staring into that darkness at his snarling face was almost worse. I knew it was crazy, but what if his expression had changed? What if he was *grinning* at me? What if he attacked me again?

My foot shot out and kicked the bag as if it were a soccer ball. I put everything I had into that kick, and my backpack went flying, landing with a *whump* at the bottom of the hole. Mom would be furious when she saw the bag was missing—it was almost new, and like she never tired of reminding me, we weren't made of money. But she would forgive me eventually. It was better this way, even if I had to carry my books in a paper bag next year. Once Edgar was gone, things would return to normal in our house, and that was worth sacrificing a backpack.

We filled that hole in record time. Scrambling through the junkyard, we hurried to the fence and freedom. The trip back to Sean's was a lot faster than getting to the landfill had been. We lifted our butts off our seats and pedaled like mad. Only when we'd reached the intersection of Willow Street and Forty-Fifth did we stop to catch our breath. Sean grinned.

"That was craptastic!"

I felt better than I had in a long time. My smile was so wide it threatened to split my face. Popping a wheelie, I tore off down the sidewalk, knowing that Sean would not be far behind. Soon he was popping wheelies too, as we competed to see who could stay aloft the longest.

We almost passed his house, barely able to skid to a stop. Our tortured tires left black, rubbery streaks on his driveway.

"Wow…we're really going to catch it," Sean said. He was staring at my pants, which were covered by a wide variety of the most foul-smelling garbage on the planet. Fortunately, his mom was still working the weekend shift, and we were able to slip inside the house without anyone noticing. While music blared through Sean's brothers' bedroom door, we scrubbed and lathered and repeated, hoping to rid ourselves of the smell that had followed us home from the landfill.

We found some rubbing alcohol under the bathroom sink, and Sean poured it over my finger, hoping to prevent an infection. Now that I was safely away from Edgar, I could give my injuries some attention.

Deep purple rings surrounded the punctures on my finger.

"That's pretty bad, man. Maybe you should see a doctor."

I knew Sean was serious when he didn't swear. But I shook my head and instead took the Band-Aid he offered, wrapping it tightly around my finger so all I could feel was the throbbing of my own blood as it fought to get through.

When Sean's mother got home, she wrinkled her nose in spite of the showers we had taken.

"What's that awful smell? What have you boys been up to?"

"Nothing, Mom, just fooling around, you know."

"Well, whatever you were doing, please don't do it again. You both reek. You'll have to wash up before dinner or you'll stink us all out of the kitchen."

With some good-natured grumbling, we raced upstairs to take second showers. I'm not sure about Sean, but my grumbling was mostly for show. I was more than happy to be free of the smell of the landfill.

The rest of the evening was a blast. With very little arm-twisting,

Sean's mom agreed to order pizza for dinner. When the food arrived, we headed downstairs with most of the booty, some cold cans of Coke, and Sean's two little brothers. We challenged each other to games of Super Mario and watched silly movies until our sides hurt from laughing and Sean's mom sent us to bed.

This was usually the moment we held flashlights under our chins and told our best ghost stories until we were both completely freaked out, but neither of us felt like telling scary stories that night. Instead we lay in our sleeping bags on Sean's bed. (It felt more like camping if we were in our sleeping bags.) I stared at the glow-in-the-dark stars on Sean's ceiling, tucking my arms behind my head. I watched them until my eyelids got heavy and I could feel myself drift.

"Josh?"

Sean's whisper startled me awake. "Yeah?"

"That stuff today…it really happened, didn't it?"

I'd been trying not to think about it. "Yeah."

"That—that *thing*. It really bit you."

"Yeah," I said, swallowing hard.

It was quiet for a while, and just when I thought he'd fallen asleep, he whispered another question into the dark.

"So what *is* it, anyway?"

"I don't know."

My answer hung heavy in the room, and Sean asked no more questions.

After everything that had happened, I expected to have nightmares. Instead, I slept better than I had in a long time. Edgar was gone—he couldn't get me in trouble anymore. And at Sean's house I was safe from

Michael too. I only hoped he hadn't taken his foul mood out on my mom.

At some point in the middle of the night, I could have sworn I heard someone whispering my name.

I decided it was a dream.

Chapter Nine

The next day I was scared to go home. Edgar may have been gone, but I still had to deal with Michael, who would be furious at how we'd taken off on him. I shuddered at the thought of what would happen if he caught me home alone.

Sean understood my plight without my saying a word. He started his campaign at breakfast, begging his mother to let me stay another night.

"Well, I don't mind, but won't your mother want you home, Josh?"

Remembering the relief in her eyes when I mentioned I'd be staying with Sean, I shook my head.

"I don't think so. I think she's glad to get me out of her hair."

Sean's mom laughed and leaned across the table to rumple my own. "I doubt that. I'll have to give her a call, but if it's all right with your mother, it's all right with me."

The possibility of being able to avoid Michael for one more day awakened my appetite, and I piled more pancakes on my plate. Sean nudged me under the table, and I glanced up to see him grinning at me. He winked, and I grinned back. Maybe his parents would adopt me, and then I could live there forever and ever. They already had three boys—what was one more? I would keep my room clean and do all the dishes. I'd be so neat they'd never know I was there. And then I wouldn't have to see Michael or worry about Edgar again.

It was a nice fantasy, but I knew it couldn't work. I couldn't leave my mother alone with *him*. Two days was one thing, but a lifetime? Never.

Sean's mother called for him when we were up in his tree house, drinking Kool-Aid and reading about the latest adventures of Spider-Man. My friend poked his head through the trapdoor.

"No moms allowed!" he roared. Ordinarily this made her smile, but not today.

"I'm sorry, boys," she said, and she really did sound sorry, "but you're going to have to come down. Josh's mother wants him home right away."

Goose bumps broke out on my arms in spite of the warmth of the day.

"But why?" Sean said in his best whiny voice. When it came to getting his way, he was an expert.

"That's what I want to talk to you about. I need you to come down here right now."

"But—"

"*Now,* Sean."

Resigned, we slumped down the ladder to the ground. By that point, my legs were trembling so badly that my sneakers kept slipping on the rungs. I almost fell twice. With our heads bowed, we dragged ourselves to where Mrs. Barry was waiting in the kitchen. She was frowning. I had never seen her so angry before.

"Is it true you were rude to Josh's stepfather?" She glared at Sean. We both started at the question. We hadn't been expecting it.

"No," Sean said, his eyes widening until he was the picture of innocence. "No, Mom. I wasn't rude to him."

"Well, Josh's mother tells it differently. She says Michael told you both to go home, and that you deliberately disobeyed him. He says that you rode off on your bicycles while he was still talking to you, and not only that—he says you went to the landfill."

Sean and I stared at each other, shocked. *How did he know?*

"Sean, you know the landfill is off-limits. How many times must I repeat myself?"

My friend hung his head, not bothering to lie. "Sorry Mom," he mumbled.

"You're lucky Josh was able to stay over here last night. His stepfather is furious. He was of half a mind to come over here and drag Josh home."

My hands went cold. I could think of nothing worse than being alone with Michael in his hearse.

"But we didn't do anything wrong! He's lying," Sean blurted. I could see the color rising in his cheeks. Soon his face would be the same shade of red as his hair. Sean was never one to stay quiet when confronted with injustice. He was kind of like a superhero that way.

"Sean…" Mrs. Barry said in her warning voice. She didn't get angry often, but when she did, she was more than a match for her son's temper. "You shouldn't say such things about Josh's stepfather."

"Yes I should! You don't know what he's like, Mom. He's…he's…" Sean struggled to find the words. "He's *evil.*"

"Okay, that's enough. You need to treat Josh's parents with respect if you want to keep playing together."

I was sure Sean's look of horror matched my own. *If* we wanted to keep playing together? Would Michael really try to keep us apart? Would my mother actually let him do it?

Mrs. Barry ran a hand through her curly hair and sighed. She wasn't happy about the situation, but I didn't think she was angry with us anymore. "Josh, your stepfather was going to come over and get you…"

I inched toward the door. I'd already decided that I was not getting into that hearse. Michael could search all over town for me if he wanted. Maybe I'd run away. I didn't want to leave my mom, but it had been her choice to let that monster into our lives.

"…But I insisted on bringing you myself, so I'm going to drive you. We can put your bike on the rack. Sean, you're going to stay here and take care of your brothers, okay?"

If I'd been facing a firing squad, I could not have felt any more doomed. I dragged myself upstairs to Sean's room. I did not want to go home. I didn't want to deal with whatever punishment Michael might be planning.

Sean patted my shoulder. "Hey man, don't worry. It'll be okay. Your mom won't let him do anything too bad."

I hadn't told him about the beatings, or the ice-water baths. I hadn't told anyone.

Mrs. Barry was quiet as we loaded my bike onto the rack on the roof of the family station wagon. I gave Sean one last goodbye. I had this awful feeling I wasn't going to see him again. I held out my hand, and he seized it, pumping it wildly.

"I'll see you tomorrow," he said, and the words had weight, like a promise. I nodded, though I wasn't at all sure that I would.

"Yeah, see you tomorrow. Thanks."

Sitting in the front seat beside Sean's mom was a little awkward. I'd known her for pretty much all my life, but Sean always sat in the front, filling the car with his chatter and jokes. All that filled it now was an uncomfortable silence.

Mrs. Barry seemed tense. Her lips were drawn into a thin line, and she was holding the steering wheel so tightly her knuckles were white. She must have been really mad at us.

We were a few blocks away from my house when she pulled into the parking lot of the local McDonald's, surprising me. We'd just eaten a gazillion pancakes, which were now a heavy lump in my stomach. I didn't think I could manage anything else.

I was about to ask if she was still hungry when she turned to me with a serious expression on her face. Usually Sean's mom was like my friend—always joking around. I'd never seen her so upset.

"Josh, is something going on at home?" Her voice was soft and careful, as if I were a deer that would spook at the slightest hint of danger. I couldn't have been more startled if she'd struck me.

"W-what do you mean?"

"I've known you since you were a wee one, Josh Leary, and I can tell something's wrong. Something's changed."

What could I say? I never expected her to ask me this question. I couldn't tell anyone about Michael and his punishments—not her, not Dr. Harvey, not my teacher. Not even Sean.

"I'm fine. I just don't want to go home, is all."

She stared out the windshield at the parking lot. Her hands still gripped the steering wheel.

"Your mother's acting different too. When I talked to her on the phone, she *said* you had to come home, but I had this feeling she really wanted me to keep you at our place. Do you know what I mean?"

Her sharp green eyes examined my face. Sean had told me that you couldn't hide things from his mother. I was really scared. What if she figured out my secret? What would happen to our family then? I lowered my gaze to my lap, unable to meet her eyes.

"Not really," I mumbled.

Mrs. Barry took my chin in her hand and lifted it so I was forced to look at her. "It's that stepfather of yours, isn't it? What is he doing to you?"

Ashamed, I pulled away from her and brushed the tears from my eyes with the back of my hand. "Nothing."

"Josh, you're not going to get in trouble. I want to help you, but you have to talk to me. Does your stepfather hurt you? Is he hurting your mom?"

As she spoke, I stole a glance at her and realized something amazing. Sean's mom didn't like Michael. She didn't like him at all.

I could feel the words bubbling up in my chest, threatening to escape. I *wanted* to tell her. I could picture the police coming for Michael and taking him away so he would never hurt us again. But what would happen afterward? Mom had told me often enough that without Michael's money, we'd be in the poorhouse. I didn't know where the poorhouse was, but Mom seemed terrified of it. It had to be pretty bad if it was worse than living with Michael.

And what if the police didn't come for my stepfather? Or worse, what if they only gave him a warning? He would kill me. No, as nice as Mrs. Barry was, I couldn't tell her.

"No, he's okay," I said.

She waited for another long moment, and then patted my hand. "If you ever decide you want to talk about it, you can call me. Anytime, day or night, do you understand?"

I nodded, not able to speak over the lump that had formed in my throat.

"And in the meantime, you can stay with us. As much as you like, as much as your mom will let you, okay?"

She started the car then, and I was relieved. Even though I really didn't want to go home, I wasn't sure I could have kept quiet much longer.

"I'm going to tell you something important, and I don't want you to forget it. If something happens at home and you need to get away, I want you to come over as fast as you can. Run straight to our house. Don't bother calling, just come. It doesn't matter how early it is, or how late. Okay?"

Surprised, I nodded again. Only when she was satisfied that I'd understood did she pull out of the parking lot. I could have sworn she muttered, *"Poor little lad."* Thoughts raced through my head as she drove closer and closer to my house. How had she known something was wrong? What had given it away? Michael had always been careful not to leave any marks. What had she seen? Did Sean know?

When she pulled into my driveway, she patted my leg briskly. She was back to her no-nonsense self. The softness she'd shown in the McDonald's parking lot was gone.

She didn't say much as she helped me get my bike off the rack. By the time we were finished, my mother had opened the front door. My heart sank as I saw how sad she looked. She was thinner than ever. Her face was pale, and there were dark smudges under her eyes. As she stood in the driveway, wringing her hands and apologizing to Sean's mother again and again for the inconvenience, I realized it was obvious there was something wrong. We might as well have posted signs in the yard.

Mrs. Barry turned to my mother then, her eyes flashing. Mom took a step back, and I didn't blame her.

"Now, I don't mean to tell you your business, Eileen. But I talked to the boys, and they said they didn't do anything wrong. I have to say I believe them. That man of yours scared the bejesus out of them. I think they've been punished enough, don't you?"

I wasn't sure what she meant. Up to that point, we hadn't been punished at all, unless taking me home was our punishment. And we *had* disobeyed my stepfather.

There was a threat to her words. I heard it, and I knew my mom heard it too. She put a hand on my shoulder, and I could feel how unsteady it was. "Yes," she said in this choked little voice that didn't sound like my mother at all. She couldn't meet Mrs. Barry's eyes either.

Sean's mom watched us for a moment. I could tell she didn't want to leave. For a minute, I thought she'd tell my mom to get in the car. Maybe Mom would agree, and Mrs. Barry would whisk us away from here. We'd live at her house and never have to see Michael again.

But that didn't happen. Instead Mrs. Barry sighed, an exasperated sound. "Well, have a good day, then. Josh, I hope I'll see you tomorrow?"

I glanced up at my mom, knowing she was being put on the spot and hoping that she'd cave. "We'll see," she said. "He has some chores to do, and he needs to apologize to his stepfather first."

Apologize to Michael? I could think of nothing I'd rather do less. But the answer seemed to satisfy Sean's mom, because she told us goodbye and got in her car. As she backed down our driveway, it took every inch of willpower not to run after her.

Once she was gone, I asked my mom the question I'd been dreading. "Is—is he really mad?"

"I don't think so. But he thought that you should come home, and I agree." She knelt down in front of me then, holding me by the arms. "Josh, I want us to be a family. A *happy* family. Michael has promised to never, ever hurt you again, but I need you to show him some respect. Do you think you can do that? Can you do it for me?"

I said I would, although I knew I'd never respect that monster, no matter what he did. And as for never hurting me again, I'd believe it when I saw it.

We walked into the house together, her arm wrapped tightly across my shoulders. If she'd noticed I no longer had a backpack or her spade, she didn't mention it.

Michael was in the living room reading a newspaper. He was sitting in my dad's recliner, and the sight of him in that chair made me furious. I wanted to hit him, to hurt him. I didn't want him anywhere near my dad's things.

He put down his paper as we came in, acting like he just realized I was home, although he must have heard Mrs. Barry's car in the driveway. Maybe he'd even heard what she'd said.

"Hello, Josh. How was the sleepover?" He flashed one of his shark-like smiles.

"Fine."

"Glad to hear it. Your little friend there, he seems like he has lots of energy."

I could feel my cheeks getting hot. "His name is Sean."

"Ah yes, that's right—*Sean*. He's a jumpy fellow, isn't he?"

I didn't know what to say. I'd thought Michael would be furious about the way we'd taken off on him. What was with this phony nice-guy act? It was even creepier than when he was holding me under water.

"Well," he said, shaking out his newspaper when I didn't respond, "I guess you better get going. You have a lot of work to do before you can see your friend again."

I stared at Mom in confusion. *What was he talking about?* I had chores to do now and then, but nothing too serious. Nothing that couldn't be finished in an hour or two.

"It's your room," she told me. "I don't know what you've done in there, but it stinks to high heaven."

My room? My room had been fine when I'd left for my adventure with Sean. Suspicious, I immediately looked over at Michael, and of course he was smirking at me.

"You have to learn to take better care of your things," he said. "Unless you want to be grounded for life."

With a sinking feeling, I ran for my room. As soon as I yanked the door open, it hit me. The smell was overpowering. Still clinging to the doorknob, I stumbled back a few steps.

My entire room was filled with the stench of ripe, rotting garbage. But that wasn't the worst of it.

There on my pillow, still covered in coffee grounds, egg shells, and God knows what else, was Edgar.

And he was grinning at me.

Chapter Ten

"But that's impossible! You're shitting me, right?"

"No," I whispered into the phone, glancing over my shoulder even though my bedroom door was closed. I'd opened the windows to let the cool air in, but the room still smelled. I was getting used to it, though. "He's definitely back."

"B-but how?" Sean's voice cracked, and I could tell he was scared.

"Michael must have followed us. He must have seen what we did, and then dug Edgar up after we left."

"That's impossible," Sean said again. "We lost him, remember? He wasn't following us. There's no way he could have turned around in time to see where we went."

"Then maybe he guessed. In a car, he could have caught up to us easy."

I shuddered at the thought of Michael waiting in the trees, watching everything we did.

"How would he have known we were going to the dump? It doesn't make sense."

"It's the *only* thing that makes sense," I insisted, and Sean must have understood, because he stopped arguing with me. The idea of Michael spying on us was creepy, but neither one of us wanted to consider the alternative.

"Where is he?" Now Sean was whispering too.

"Who, Michael?"

"The *bear*, you idiot. Where is that butt-sucking bear?"

"In the washing machine. He was all covered with crap." I wrinkled my nose at the memory. Mom had been all too happy to see that I was finally doing some laundry. Thankfully she hadn't seen what I was washing. She would not have been impressed by Edgar's current state.

"He didn't bite you or anything?"

"I didn't give him a chance." I'd thrown a sheet over the bear, much like I'd throw a butterfly net over a frog. What if he struggled? What if I *saw* him struggle? Seeing something like that would make me lose my mind. But Edgar hadn't stirred. He'd acted like any other dumb teddy bear, even when I threw the laundry soap in his face.

"Good. Maybe the little piss-arse will drown."

"I don't think so," I said, but I hoped the same. Every time I thought of Edgar down there in the basement, going through the spin cycle, I pictured that terrible sneer. Edgar was still alive, all right. Alive and planning his revenge.

"So we'll drown him. You're not grounded anymore, right? Your room is clean now, right?"

The smell of garbage had been so strong that I doubted it would go away. I'd borrowed some of Mom's lavender potpourri, but that had only made it worse. Now my room stunk of rot and flowers. In spite of the stench, it was as clean as it had ever been. My clothes and toys were picked up, and the floor sparkled. "Yeah."

"Meet me tomorrow at the lake. And bring Edgar. Be prepared to say goodbye to that bastard bear."

I couldn't help hoping that my friend's plan would work. But even then, I had my doubts.

Edgar more than survived his laundry room experience—he thrived. With his fur all fluffy and clean, he seemed new again. If it weren't for the snarl that twisted his snout, he would have been almost cute. He still stunk, though.

I was tempted to throw him in the closet where Michael kept all of his things, but if Sean's plan was going to work, I'd need the bear first thing tomorrow morning. However, that wasn't the only reason I kept Edgar with me. I didn't want him anywhere near my mother.

Still, I wasn't taking any chances. The entire time Edgar had been in the wash, I'd been plotting. Now that he was back in my room, I worked fast. I wrapped a skipping rope around the teddy bear, pinning its arms to its sides. I wound duct tape around his snout, feeling a little guilty. I knew it was silly, but what if Edgar needed to breathe? What if I was killing him? I saw fear in the teddy bear's eyes and almost released him before I remembered the tacks in my feet. I had to be strong. When it came to Edgar, it was definitely a case of kill or be killed. Besides, he was just a teddy bear. It wasn't like he was *alive* or anything. No living creature could survive over an hour in the washing machine and dryer.

Once everything that could hurt me was either tied down or covered, I threw the teddy bear into a pillowcase, which I knotted at the top. Then I grabbed my dad's big metal toolbox, which was so heavy I could barely lift it. I'd emptied the tools into a drawer in the garage while Edgar was having his bath. The toolbox was perfect, because it had a lock.

I stuffed Edgar into the bottom, squeezing and pushing his repulsively soft body until it fit. Sliding the two metal trays into place over him, I slammed the toolbox shut and locked it. I put the key on a piece of twine and tied the twine around my neck like a necklace, tucking the key under my shirt. I wasn't taking any chances. Even if Michael knew where to look, there was no way he'd be able to rescue Edgar without my noticing.

I was safe. For that night at least.

I woke up gasping for air. The room flooded with light. I rolled over on my side, coughing and choking. My throat burned.

"Josh, are you all right? What's wrong?"

I could feel my mother's hands on my shoulders and hear the fear in her voice. I couldn't stop coughing, and I couldn't get enough air.

"I can't breathe," I managed to wheeze. All I knew was that I'd woken up feeling like something was strangling me. I'd tried to inhale, but nothing happened. My hands had flown up to my throat, where they scrabbled at the plastic cord that was embedded deep in my skin, but I couldn't get it loose. Pinpricks of light exploded in the darkness in front of my eyes, and I knew I was going to die. With my last bit of strength, I punched and kicked as hard as I could, and suddenly the pressure on my throat eased. That's when I screamed.

"Oh my God—what happened to your neck? What on earth?" Mom lifted something from my bed. Now that I was somewhat accustomed to the light, I could see what she was holding.

My blood ran cold.

It was my skipping rope, the rope I'd tied around Edgar.

Edgar, who was now resting on my pillow, grinning, his snout slightly sticky from the duct tape.

I spent the rest of the night on the couch.

Sean's eyes were as big as baseballs when he saw my neck. "What in the bloody blazes of ass happened to you?"

I wanted to tell him, but Mom was nearby. I couldn't see her, but I could feel her presence. She'd been hovering over me since last night. She too wanted to know what had happened, but I couldn't tell her the truth—she'd think I was crazy. The last time I was honest with her, she'd made me see Dr. Harvey.

I shook my head slightly to let him know I couldn't talk. Sean understood immediately, and after scanning the living room to make sure the coast was clear, he mouthed, "The bear?"

I tilted my head toward the duffel bag that rested on the couch. It had been my dad's, an old bag that he'd used to carry camping gear. I didn't think anyone would miss it, but I was running out of bags. Hopefully this would be the last one I'd waste on Edgar.

"Mom! We're leaving now," I yelled, trying to make it seem like I actually believed she wasn't around the corner, listening. Sure enough, she was instantly in the room with us.

"I'm not sure it's such a good idea to go out today, Josh. You're hurt."

"I'm fine, Mom," I said, putting on a big show of acting embarrassed in front of Sean. *Don't baby me,* my eyes pleaded. My throat was a bit sore, and my voice sounded funny, but otherwise it was like nothing had happened. As long as you ignored the ugly purple marks on my neck.

"Where are you planning to go?" Her eyes flicked from my face to Sean's. Sean widened his eyes and tried his best to appear innocent, as always.

"The lake," I said, as if it were obvious.

"The lake again? Didn't you go there yesterday?"

"We like the lake, Mrs. Leary," Sean said.

"Yeah, we like the lake, Mom."

Her eyes narrowed in suspicion. "Are you *sure* you're going to the lake? Michael said he saw you near the Industrial Park yesterday, and that's nowhere near it."

For a moment, my mind went blank. I had absolutely no idea what to tell her, but thankfully Sean piped up. "It was the storm, Mrs. Leary. When it started raining, we decided to go to my friend's place instead."

Mom's forehead creased in confusion. "What storm? There was no storm that day."

Sean and I stared at each other in surprise. "You didn't hear it? All the thunder and lightning?" I asked.

"It was pouring, Mrs. Leary," Sean added.

"Well, it wasn't raining here," Mom said, crossing her arms. I could tell by her expression that she was having a hard time believing us, but why would we lie about a storm? "You know I don't like you riding in the rain, Josh. If this storm was so bad, why didn't you come straight home?"

"My friend's place was closer," Sean said.

The three of us were silent a minute while Mom studied our faces for signs of deception. Finally, she sighed. "All right, you can go to the lake. But I want you to actually go to the lake—nowhere else. And I want you home by dinner, no excuses. Okay?"

Sean broke into a huge, reassuring grin. "I'll make sure of it, Mrs. Leary," he promised, and my mother couldn't help but smile in return. Sean had that effect on parents, especially mothers.

A great wave of relief washed over me. If Sean felt confident enough to promise my mother that we'd be back by dinner, that meant his plan wouldn't take very long. Before the day was over, I'd be rid of Edgar again.

I hoped.

Chapter Eleven

This time we'd come prepared. Though there wasn't a cloud in the sky, we'd both worn our rain jackets. Sean had his father's pocketknife tucked into his jeans in case there were more snakes, but we needn't have worried. The ride to the lake was uneventful. I'd stuffed the duffel bag in my bike basket, but the bear never moved. Maybe he was tired from trying to kill me the night before. Whatever the reason, it was a good sign.

A blond teenager was skipping stones across the water when we arrived. As soon as he heard us coming, he stalked toward us with a scowl on his face.

"Where have you been?" he snarled. "You told me you were going to be here half an hour ago."

My hands tightened on my handlebars as I prepared to hightail it out of there. The kid seemed like trouble. But Sean wasn't concerned.

"Sorry, man," he said with a shrug. "We got held up."

The teenager glanced at me, and his eyes widened. "What the hell happened to you?"

"His T-shirt was too tight," Sean said before I could open my mouth. "What do you care?"

The guy continued to look me over as if he was afraid I might attack. Then he sneered. "I want to get out of here, okay? I've got better things to do. Have you got it?"

Sean lowered his bike to the ground and walked over to the kid, digging in his pockets as he went. I was shocked when he withdrew a handful of crumpled bills—more money than I'd seen in my life—and thrust it at the stranger, who counted it carefully.

"Okay," he said when he was satisfied. "Where is it?"

"Can you give us a couple of minutes? Just a couple. It's not quite ready."

"Okay," the kid said, clearly exasperated with my friend. "But hurry up. I don't have all day."

Sean seized the duffel bag from my basket. "Come on," he said. "We don't have much time."

As I followed him, my mind was flooded with questions. Who was the kid? What was the money for? What was Sean's plan? But I could tell my friend wasn't in the mood for talking. He threw the bag down by a pile of stones and zipped it open. I flinched, but Edgar was still wrapped in one of my old T-shirts. He looked like a bunch of laundry.

Sean threw stones into the bag as fast as he could. "Take the biggest ones that'll fit. We gotta make sure this monkey ass-loving mofo sinks."

I grabbed the largest stones I could handle and tossed them into the bag. Within a couple of minutes, the duffel was so full that we could barely zip it back up. Edgar was completely covered with rocks. It took both of us to lug the bag to the teenager, who stood there smirking at us.

"Whatcha got there, a body?"

"Our deal was no questions." Sean panted, dropping the bag at the boy's feet. He seemed as exhausted as I felt. There'd been no time to recover from the other day's adventure. If this one didn't work, we were screwed.

The kid pouted. "I have a right to know what I'm taking. I don't want to be involved in anything illegal."

"It's not illegal. Just some old stuff of his stepfather's," Sean said, gesturing at me. I glared back as the teenager gave me another cold once-over.

"Your stepfather do that to you?" he asked, pointing to my neck. I nodded. Maybe this guy would be more willing to help us if he knew what kind of man my stepfather was.

The teen turned his attention back to Sean, the threat clear in his voice. "If this guy comes after you, I don't want my name mentioned, okay? I want no part of this."

"What do we seem like, rats? We're not going to say anything." Sean held the older kid's gaze bravely, but when the teenager finally picked up the duffel bag, my friend's shoulders sagged with relief. I was pleased to see the older kid could hardly lift it.

"Jesus Christ! This is overkill, isn't it?"

For a minute, I was terrified he would refuse to take it, but he hefted the bag in his arms, muttering something about sinking and how he would make sure Sean paid for it.

He walked toward the water with the bag. We followed close behind. Once we'd cleared the trees, I spotted something I hadn't noticed when we'd first arrived. Sitting on the grass was a bright red canoe. The teenager tossed the bag in the boat, and I got chills when I heard the hollow thunk.

"Can I get a little help here?" he said, and we hurried to the back of the canoe, pushing it across the grass to the banks of the lake. Once the boat's nose was in the water, the teenager took a paddle out of the canoe and climbed inside. Sweat trickled down my spine as I waited to see what would happen.

The teenager winked at Sean, smiling for the first time. "Pleasure doing business with you, Barry." He pushed off, his tan arms guiding the paddle smoothly through the water. Sean and I stood on the banks of the lake and watched in horrified fascination.

"We shouldn't let him take Edgar, Sean." I whispered, though the kid was too far away to hear us by now. "What if something happens to him?"

"It couldn't happen to a nicer guy. Trust me. Will's a scumbag."

"But what's he doing? What's the plan?"

"He's taking him to the deepest part of the lake. Even if Edgar can swim, he's not coming back from that. That bear's days are over." He pointed at my neck. "I wish I could say the same for your stepfather, but you heard the kid—no illegal stuff."

"You know my stepfather didn't do this." I brought my hand self-consciously to my throat. Judging by the looks I was getting, the bruise must have darkened.

"I know, but it's his bear. And I think he gave it to you for a reason, you know?"

The same thing had occurred to me many times. Michael had known exactly what he was doing.

Will and his canoe were a bright speck in the distance now. He was making good time. Around us, families laughed and chatted, spreading blankets for picnics and playing games of touch football and Frisbee. It was a beautiful sunny day. There was no sign of impending doom, but I couldn't take my eyes off Will—or the sky. Any moment now, it would happen. The clouds would open up and rain would pour down on us, soaking everyone to the skin. Or maybe Will's boat would spring a leak. *Something* had to happen. It couldn't be this easy.

"Woo-hoo! I think he's stopping!" Sean said, peering through a pair of G.I. Joe binoculars. "Yep, he's got the bag. He's tossing it over now."

"Is everything okay? The boat's not sinking or anything?"

He handed me the binoculars. "See for yourself."

It took me a second to adjust the focus. Sean was near-sighted but he'd never admit it. He said only nerds wore glasses. By the time I could see Will clearly, he was already on his way back. There was no sign of the duffel bag. "I can't believe it," I said, handing the binoculars back to Sean. I was expecting a lake monster to lurch out of the depths and devour Will, canoe and all.

Sean brushed the dirt from his hands. "Well, that's done. No need to wait around. What do you want to do now?"

I looked back at the lake and the red canoe that was getting closer and closer. "Shouldn't we wait for him?"

"Nah. He's got his money; we're rid of the bear. What else is there to say?"

"I don't get it. Why was it so hard for us, and so easy for him?"

Sean grinned at the crowd around us. A mother smiled back, unable to resist my friend's charms. "Witnesses, my friend. It's all about the witnesses."

It was true. Whenever Edgar had hurt me or destroyed stuff, no one was around. Sean had seen the worst of him during that terrifying trip to the landfill, but for the most part, Edgar only attacked when I was alone. There was no way he'd do anything to Will with all these people watching.

"Thanks, Sean."

"Hey, no problem, buddy." He slung an arm around my shoulders. "Let's celebrate. How about a swim, followed by some ice cream?"

It was much too soon to celebrate, but we didn't know that yet.

Chapter Twelve

"Well, you're home early." My mom stood up from her flowerbed and smiled. I hadn't seen her this happy in a long time. Maybe she could tell that Edgar was gone. It was like the shadow had lifted from our house. "The sun's still out."

"You wanted me home for dinner." With the way things had been lately, I only came home when she insisted. I would have much rather eaten dinner at Sean's.

"About that…what would you think of hotdogs?"

"Hotdogs, really?" I felt like I'd won the lottery. Hotdogs were a special treat, especially after Michael had moved in with us. Since he'd started his diet, he shunned anything he considered junk food, and hotdogs were definitely on the list.

"Do you want them with beans or with mac and cheese?"

"Mac and cheese!" I cried, but I knew she was asking to tease me. I'd eat Kraft Macaroni and Cheese every night if I could.

"Okay, on one condition."

I groaned, but just because it was expected of me. I knew whatever she wanted wouldn't be so bad. When she was in a good mood, she was easy to please. "I should have known."

"You have to wash up. And that means a proper bath, Josh. None of this splashing around in the sink and telling me you've cleaned up."

"But that *is* cleaning up," I protested. What is it about mothers and baths? If they had their way, we'd spend our whole lives in the tub.

"No deals. Take a bath, or it's liver and onions for dinner."

"You never make liver and onions. You don't even *like* liver and onions." I knew she was still teasing me, but I also knew she'd end up getting me to take a bath. Mom was relentless in her own way.

"So I'll start. You better head up," she said, gesturing to the house with another spade. She hadn't asked me about the other one yet, the one I'd borrowed. "There's not much time until dinner."

"But Mom…I was just in the lake for hours."

"Even more reason to take a bath." Mom wrinkled her nose. "You don't know what's in that water. You know how many kids pee in there?"

I knew when to accept defeat. Trying not to think of the answer to her question, I broke into a run, making it to the house in record time. I'd have the fastest bath in the history of the world. It wouldn't be so bad. And even better…

If we were having hotdogs for dinner, it could only mean one thing. Michael wasn't home.

It wasn't that I hated baths, exactly—it was just that they seemed like such a waste of time. There was always something else I'd much rather do. Mom used to let me take showers until she realized that the two minutes I spent under the water wasn't enough time to get *anything* clean. She'd promised me I could go back to showers when I turned thirteen. By then, she said, I'd have gotten the hang of it.

Our tub was actually kind of cool, for a bathtub. Mom said it had come with the house, so that meant it was over a hundred years old. It had feet like a dragon's, and it was deeper than some kids' wading pools.

I used to love to sail boats in it when I was little. Now I hated how long it took to fill.

Grabbing Mom's bar of pink soap, I scrubbed all of the lake gunk off my skin. The water turned brown around my feet, which were filthy from running on the muddy banks with no shoes. As much as I hated to admit it, maybe Mom did have a point. I slipped beneath the water for a moment, closing my eyes. I wasn't in a hurry to get out any longer. It would be a few minutes before dinner was ready, and the warm water felt so good.

When my chest grew tight from the lack of air, I tried to let myself float back to the surface. But something was wrong. I wasn't floating...it felt like I was pinned down.

My pulse was thudding in my ears. My eyes flew open. Edgar was leering down at me from the edge of the tub. I knew it was him, even though he was soaked and covered with slimy lake weeds. My mouth opened to scream, and I choked on the dirty, soapy water.

I thrashed and struggled, fighting to sit up, but it was like invisible hands were pressing down on my chest. The urge to breathe was irresistible, but I knew that if I took a breath underwater, I would die. My chest grew tight and painful. A snarl twisted Edgar's muzzle, but his yellow eyes glowed with happiness. I realized he wanted to see me die. Nothing else would satisfy him.

My legs were growing weak, but I flailed them around as much as I could, hoping Mom would hear the splashing and come to see what was wrong. I was feeling dizzy now. With what was left of my strength, I shot out my hand and knocked Edgar off the side of the tub. Suddenly, the pressure on my chest was gone. I burst out of the water, gasping for air. Soap burned my eyes, and I swiped at them with my hands, only to pull back when I realized something was still wrong. My hands were *slimy*.

In a panic, I hurried to get out of the tub. I didn't know where Edgar was, and for a moment, I didn't care if I stepped on him. When I got the soap out of my eyes so I could finally see the water, I wanted to puke.

The tub was full of the same disgusting lake weeds that had been wrapped around the bear. Water worms writhed, along with the occasional leech. Hopping around the room, I swiped at my hair and skin like someone possessed. A fat leech clung to my leg, and with a grimace, I used a tissue to pull it from my skin and flush it down the toilet. Blood ran down my leg where its teeth had sunk in.

I scanned the room for Edgar, but he was gone. That left the problem of the tub. How on earth was I going to get all that stuff out of there without Mom finding out? I stared at the worms squiggling through the water and shuddered. Using the handle of the toilet plunger, I hammered on the tub's plug until it released. You couldn't have paid me to reach into that water.

"Josh, did you die in there? Dinner is ready."

Almost, I thought. I'd almost died. Edgar was playing for keeps, and I might not best him the next time. I couldn't go to sleep knowing he was in the house somewhere. Somehow, I'd have to end this tonight.

"I'm okay, but…can you bring me some paper towels? I have to clean out the tub." I'd been afraid I wouldn't be able to speak, but I sounded fine, if a little hoarse.

I could sense Mom's hesitation from the other side of the door. "Clean the tub? Josh, are you feeling okay?"

"Yeah. It's just—I had some lake goo on me and stuff. It's kind of gross."

She sighed. "Now do you understand why I don't like you swimming in there? God knows what kind of parasites are in that water."

"Don't worry, Mom," I said, staring at the mess that awaited me at the bottom of the tub. "I don't think I'll go swimming there again."

"Well, don't worry about it now. I'll clean it up after dinner. You should eat while the food's still hot."

"NO!" I sounded more frantic than I'd meant, but I knew I'd never be able to explain the disaster in her bathroom. If she saw this mess, she'd know I couldn't have carried all that stuff in on my body. And if she found out the truth about Edgar—the *real* truth—she'd never be able to handle it. "I don't want you to see it. *Please*, Mom."

She was silent for a moment. I leaned my head against the bathroom door and shut my eyes. I was so tired and weak I could barely stand. I couldn't keep up the fight much longer. If she insisted on cleaning it up herself...

"You must be the only ten-year-old boy in the history of the world who's begged to clean the bathroom. If I get you the paper towels and some cleaner, do you promise me you'll hurry and come down when you're done?"

I exhaled in relief—I hadn't realized I'd been holding my breath. "Yeah."

It took me ten minutes to mop all the squirming goop out of the tub. My stomach churned as I squelched the worms and weeds between wads of paper towel. I used the whole roll and filled the garbage bag. When I was done, I insisted on taking the trash out to the curb—I didn't want Mom peeking inside.

She wasn't pleased when I could hardly choke down any supper, but I'd lost my appetite.

I had a job to do, and there was no time to waste. I had to get it done before Michael came home.

Chapter Thirteen

I should have done this from the start. I'm not sure why I didn't.

Finding Edgar was easy. He was on my pillow, just as I had expected. When I opened my bedroom door, the metallic smell of lake water filled my nose and I gagged. If I never saw the lake again, it would be too soon.

Edgar's eyes shone as he watched me cling to the doorframe, coughing and hacking. I could have sworn he was smiling at me.

"Go ahead, smile while you still can, you cocksucking mofo," I growled, using the very best of Sean's swears. "You and me are done."

I threw a garbage bag over Edgar before I could second-guess myself. This time he fought like a wildcat, kicking and clawing and growling. Scratches and then holes appeared in the bag, which was thrashing around so much I had a hard time holding it. I'd come prepared, though, and threw the bag with Edgar into another, stronger bag.

I think he knew it was over. He was fighting for his life.

Edgar howled, a sickening sound that twisted my insides into knots. I paused for a moment, worried. Surely my mom would hear him, and then what? What could I possibly tell her? But no one came.

I slipped out the door, carrying the bag. The bag, and a metal container of lighter fluid in one of my pockets. Several books of matches were in the other. I wasn't taking any chances.

Like most houses in town, we had a burning barrel in the backyard.

We burned what trash we could at home to save on trips to the dump. I should have used it a long time ago, except...

I guess there was a part of me that shied away from burning something that seemed to be alive, even an evil bear like Edgar.

I threw everything into the barrel—the bag of mess from the tub and the bag with the bear, which was still going crazy. The adrenaline racing through my body made me shaky, but I managed to empty the entire can of lighter fluid over the bags. My trembling fingers struck a match. It briefly flared to life, but then went out. That was okay. I had more where that came from, and I knew where Mom kept Dad's old Zippo.

The back door creaked open. "Josh, what on earth are you doing? You're not supposed to..."

Woosh! The book of matches in my hand caught fire, and I tossed them into the burning barrel. Flames burst high into the sky, and I fell backward onto the grass. It was over. It was finally over.

Mom ran from the house to help me. "Are you okay?"

I couldn't help smiling at her. "I'm great."

The fire roared and crackled, sending a shower of sparks sizzling to the ground. Mom pulled me to my feet. Once she had us safely out of range, she turned on me.

"You know I don't like you fooling around with matches, Joshua Leary. What on earth did you put in there?"

I shrugged. "Just some garbage."

I was having a nightmare. Someone was screaming. *Mom!* Mom was screaming.

My eyes flew open, but I immediately shut them again. The room was thick with smoke that stung my eyes and hurt my nostrils. I wheezed. I could hear an ominous crackling noise that kept getting louder and louder.

Someone pounded hard on my bedroom door, startling me. "Josh! Let us in," Michael yelled. "Don't do this, buddy. Let us help you."

I knew what to do. We'd been over this in school a hundred times. I rolled out of my bed onto the floor. Pain flared up from my hips and knees when I fell, but I didn't care. I'd realized the awful truth. My bedroom was on fire. I gasped when I saw the planks of wood nailed across my door, trapping me inside. How had Edgar managed that?

I'd been exposed to the smoke for too long already. Black spots swam in front of me. I laid my cheek against the floor, which was surprisingly cool. I closed my eyes.

"Josh, please! I can't lose you. Please open the door."

Mom's voice broke me out of my trance. I began to crawl toward my art table. I could feel the heat on my skin now. I didn't have much time. I got what oxygen was left in the room by pressing my face against the floor and inhaling as deeply as I could.

At first I was afraid Edgar would have done something to my window too, but it was clear. With my last bit of strength, I threw my desk chair at the glass. The window shattered. I gulped the fresh air gratefully, but I could feel the fire gaining strength right behind me. There was a frightful cracking noise as my door and the floor around it started to give. I couldn't hear my mom anymore.

I hoped she had gotten out in time.

I leaned out over my window. The driveway pulsed with flashing red lights from the fire trucks. The crimson glow made the faces of the firefighters seem demonic, but I recognized Mr. Gillies, the father of a girl in my class.

"Hang on, Josh," he yelled. "We're getting a ladder for you. Just hang on."

My bedroom door gave with an earsplitting crack. It sounded like it had been hit by a giant's ax. "Please hurry!" I tried to holler, but it came out as a strangled croak. No one could hear me over the roar of the flames. My eyes and throat burned with the smoke. I started coughing, and it felt like I would never stop.

I could see the firefighters running to my window with a ladder. Mr. Gillies climbed up and stretched out his arms to me. His coat was rough under my hands, but I held on as hard as I could. As we made our way down the ladder, I craned my head to stare at the gathering crowd. Still coughing and choking, I fought for air.

"Take it easy, Josh. You're safe now," Mr. Gillies said. He didn't put me down until he reached the end of the driveway.

"But where's my mom? My mom is in there!" I started to cry, and for once I didn't care who saw. I couldn't lose her after what had happened to Dad.

"Calm down, son. Your mother is fine. She's right over there."

I saw her running toward me, Michael close behind. I felt my knees buckle, and another firefighter wrapped a blanket around my shoulders. Even though it was a warm night, I was shivering.

Mom threw her arms around me and crushed me to her, sobbing. I let her hug me, watching in wonder over her shoulders as our family home burned.

"Why did you do it, Josh? Why?"

I pulled away in shock. "What do you mean? *I* didn't do anything!"

That's when I noticed the men. They were standing with Michael, speaking in the low tones adults use when they don't want you to hear.

"Mom, I didn't do this, I swear. You have to believe me!"

Tears ran down her face. "It's my fault. Michael told me you were sick, but I didn't believe it. I didn't *want* to believe it. It's all my fault, honey. I should have gotten you more help."

She tried to hug me again, but I pushed her away, which only made her cry harder. "I'm not sick. I didn't do anything wrong!" I tried to run away, but it was too late. The men surrounded me.

"Josh, you need to come with us for a bit, all right?" one of the men said. He knelt so he was at my eye level and smiled. "Don't worry. We need to take you to the hospital for a bit, make sure you're okay."

I didn't think. I just reacted. My fist shot out, and I punched that nice man in the face. I got halfway down the street before the men caught up to me. They hauled me back to the driveway while I kicked and screamed. They put me in a van with metal mesh on all the windows. I couldn't open the door from the inside, but I pounded on the glass.

"Mom, don't let them take me! It wasn't me. It was the bear! It was Edgar—"

And that's when I saw him.

My mother was huddled on the driveway, covering her face with her hands. Some of our neighbors were trying to help her stand, to pick her off the ground, but Michael wasn't paying any attention to them.

He was stroking something he held close to his chest under his coat. *Cradling* something.

I saw familiar yellow eyes glow in the night.

Edgar grinned at me.

Chapter Fourteen

I never saw my mother again. The Clear Springs Mental Hospital was my home for the next three years, but Mom never got a chance to visit. It was a freak accident, they said—some genetic time bomb no one could have predicted. Two nights after the fire, my mother's heart stopped. The doctors could say what they wanted, but I knew the truth. I pictured her opening her eyes on that final night to see Edgar looming over her. I had nightmares about it for years.

Michael tried to see me once, but Dr. Harvey told him it wasn't a good idea, and that was that. Once my stepfather got the insurance money from our house and my mother's death, he closed his funeral home and left town. Last I heard, he was somewhere in the Caribbean. I was grateful to know there was an ocean between Edgar and me.

"Honey, are you all right?" My wife put her hand on my arm. Her brow was furrowed with concern. I forced a smile.

"I'm fine. I was thinking that my mother would have loved to meet him."

She wrapped her arms around my waist and gave me a squeeze as we watched the newest member of our family. Bradley was our first child, and I was still overwhelmed by the strength of my love for him. I would never let anything bad happen to him, ever.

"I'm sorry. This is probably so hard for you." Rachel slipped under my arm and leaned her head against my shoulder. She'd been home from the hospital for only a day and was still exhausted, but true to her nature, she was wasting her time worrying about me.

"Are you kidding?" I lifted her off the ground and gave her a kiss. "This has been the best moment of my life. Nothing will spoil it for me."

I could feel her relax. "I'm glad," she said. "I was worried for a second."

"Well, you don't have to worry about me. This is what I've always wanted—to have a family again. I couldn't be happier."

Rachel smiled, tilting her head to the side as we watched our son sleep. "Isn't he an angel?"

"He is."

"We should get some sleep while we can. You know he's going to be awake again soon enough."

She walked down the hallway to our bedroom. As I was about to follow, something made me turn. I wanted to look at my son one last time.

That was when I noticed it.

There was something in the crib with my baby boy.

Something black and fluffy with yellow eyes and a sneer on its face.

Edgar had come home.

About the Author

Raised in the far north amid Jack London's world of dog sleds and dark winters, J.H. Moncrieff has been a professional writer all of her adult life.

Harlequin conducted a worldwide search for "the next Gillian Flynn" to launch their new line of psychological thrillers, and Moncrieff was one of two authors selected. This novella, *The Bear Who Wouldn't Leave,* was featured in Samhain's *Childhood Fears* collection and stayed on its horror bestsellers list for over a year.

During her years as a journalist, she tracked down snipers and canoed through crocodile-infested waters. She has published hundreds of articles in national and international magazines and newspapers.

When she's not writing, she loves to travel to exotic locations, advocate for animal rights, and muay thai kickbox.

J.H. loves to hear from her readers.

You can email her at jh@jhmoncrieff.com or connect with her on Facebook and Twitter.

Visit her website at www.jhmoncrieff.com or view the trailer for this book at https://www.youtube.com/watch?v=fl7CvUvqHdM.

Acknowledgments

The folks at Samhain Horror have been wonderful to work with. I especially thank Don D'Auria for his kindness and patience, and fellow writers J.G. Faherty and L.L. Soares for their guidance.

Being a writer is wonderful, but it can also be incredibly isolating. I'm lucky enough to have a tremendous support system, and I'd like to thank my copy editor and spouse Chris Brogden, Dee Dee Gould and Drew Kozub from my writing group, my personal cheerleaders Christine Brandt and Lisa Saunders, and all of my blog readers, friends, and family for their years of encouragement.

Drew and his partner in crime, Jarrod Tully, are responsible for the awesome book trailer, and I wouldn't have a website if it weren't for my friend and designer extraordinaire Kyla Roma. I'm truly blessed to be surrounded by such talented people.

I'd be remiss if I didn't thank Stephen King for his masterpiece *On Writing*, which gave me the kick in the pants I needed to start writing fiction again.

Thanks for reading!

Coming soon from J.H. Moncrieff and DeathZone Books—two tales of spine-tingling supernatural suspense!

City of Ghosts & The Girl Who Talks to Ghosts
© *2017 J.H. Moncrieff*

Enjoy the following excerpt for City of Ghosts, book one in J.H. Moncrieff's new GhostWriters series:

~ Chapter One ~

It was easier than I thought.

All I had to do was bide my time in one of the less popular temples, crouching behind a weird-ass statue while the guides checked for stragglers. Thankfully, they didn't do a thorough search—just popped their bobbed heads in and glanced around before hurrying to their cozy cruise ships.

Guess I couldn't blame them. It seemed like it was always pissing down rain in this part of the country—at least, it had been since we'd been here—and even though it was mid-September, it was freaking cold.

As I stepped over the temple's sacred threshold and hurried to the place I'd chosen to camp for the night, I grinned, unable to resist pumping my fist in the air. *I'd done it. What would the group say when they realized I wasn't on the ship?*

Only the terminally stupid got left behind on a tour, so they'd probably figure I was hung over again, and in that, they'd be partially right. It takes skill to get a decent buzz on the watery crap they call beer in China, which is why I switched to the rice wine. Doesn't take much to feel it, but you pay for it the following day.

It was six p.m., but the sun was already setting. Flipping up the hood of my jacket against the drizzling rain, I whistled to keep myself company, careful not to slip on the wet stone path. The place where I'd decided to spend the night was perfect. Even though it had fallen into ruin, that particular temple still had a bit of roof left, so I'd be able to get dry. Since it was open to the air, I wouldn't have to worry about my campfire burning it down. There was enough junk in there to keep a decent fire going—not that I was worried.

It wasn't like I believed in ghosts.

I'd planned this for a long while, which is kind of out of character for me. My little sister Roxi is the planner in the family—she's always making lists and schedules and color-coded charts. I would have loved to bring her with me, but she won't go anywhere without consulting every available website about what to wear, what to pack, what to do and not do, and there wasn't time for that. The *why* of this trip was planned, but the *when* was not—it was a matter of waiting for the right seat sale, and when I found it, I pounced.

That's more my style. I prefer to just do stuff, go with the flow, see where life takes me. Problem was, for the last few years it hadn't taken me anywhere interesting.

Much like the vast majority of my peers, I'd had no clue what to do after high school. I'd gone to university because my buddies were going, and ended up drinking and partying my way through a lackluster Bachelor of Arts degree. Which qualified me to drive a cab or spout deep philosophies that annoyed the hell out of pretty much everyone. If it weren't for juggling tracks as a part-time DJ, I would have starved to death.

Since the idea of playing *The Chicken Dance* at yet another wedding made me want to hang myself, I took a two-year computer course that landed me an entry-level IT job at an insurance company. Which was about as interesting as listening to AM radio, but hey, at least I was earning decent money without having to watch a bunch of biddies flap their arms.

It was a start.

Trouble was, I was still there four years later.

So a few months ago I came up with this brilliant idea. It was so damn brilliant I didn't tell anyone about it—not even Roxi.

China has plenty of ghost cities, but I'd gone for the most infamous. The locals believed spirits actually live here. Now that Hensu was empty of tour groups, with their incessant questions and stupid umbrellas hitting me in the head every time I turned around, it had an abandoned feel that was more than a little creepy.

A figure loomed out of the darkness, brandishing a sword at my skull, and I jumped before realizing it was another statue. In the daylight, with its pig-like face and coating of moss, it had been comical. I wasn't laughing now. Why the Chinese decided to fill their ghost city with fake ghosts was beyond me. If they really believed spirits lived here, the statues were overkill.

What the Chinese call ghosts are more like demons to us. But demons, ghosts, whatever—these spirits were lifeless chunks of rock. Nothing to freak out over.

I dug a flashlight out of my pocket and clicked it on, but that just made things worse. It cast an eerie blue glow that danced in the statues eyes, turning their grins into leers.

"Chill, Jacks," I muttered to myself. "They're rocks, and you don't believe in this supernatural shit, remember?"

There was no way I was gonna drain my phone battery to see where I was going, no matter how much the blue light spooked me. What the hell was wrong with me? Why had I regressed to the age of ten? Gotta be the hangover. I had to lay off the booze. Who knew what was in that Chinese stuff? I'd probably pickled my brain.

Once I found the ruined temple again, it took me about ten minutes to scrounge enough wood for a decent fire. By then my fingers were numb with cold and my stomach was growling. There hadn't been time to grab breakfast on the ship, and I'd forfeited lunch when I'd ditched the tour. The sooner I could get a hot meal in me, the better. Maybe then I wouldn't be so damn jumpy.

Not that it was much of a meal. As the fire crackled, sending smoke swirling into the night air, I hauled out what Roxi would call "meager provisions": a handful of those neon pink sausage things that line the shelves of every Chinese grocery store. I'd bought them on a dare. No one in our tour group knew what they were made of, and honestly, I didn't *want* to know. One label showed a penguin dancing with a cob of corn. Hopefully that was a case of something getting seriously lost in translation.

I had the sausages for protein, two cans of Pringles for bulk, and a couple cans of Coke to wash it down (or kill the taste of the sausages). Chinese Pringles came in intriguing flavors like seaweed and sizzling hot pot, but I figured the sausages were adventure enough for one night. I'd grabbed two cans of good ol' sour cream and onion instead. The meat would most likely turn out to be inedible, but at least I wouldn't starve. I tried not to think about the five-course dinner the rest of my group was enjoying.

One of the rotting pieces of wood I'd stuck in the fire collapsed with a loud crackle that made me flinch. Flurries of sparks raced each other to the roof, and I watched their progress, uneasy. What if the temple caught fire? What if I burned the entire thing down? You do *not* want to be on the wrong side of the police in China. Plenty of tourists had made that mistake and they'd never been heard from again.

My guide Harold would be pissed that I'd started a fire—it's not like I'd be able to hide the evidence. Then again, since he was the one who'd abandoned me here (well, as far as he knew, anyway) I figured I'd get off easy. He couldn't expect me to freeze to death. Come to think of it, considering the expression his face twisted into whenever he was forced to acknowledge me, he probably would.

The sparks winked out before they reached the ceiling, and even if they hadn't, everything was probably soaked through from the rain. Careful to breathe through my mouth, I sliced into a sausage wrapper with my Swiss Army knife, grimacing at the slimy liquid that burst from the package. Before I could question the wisdom of this decision, I jammed the slippery contents onto a folding camp fork I'd stuffed in my daypack. Everything tastes better when it's cooked over a campfire, right? That's what I was counting on.

While I charred the hell out of the sausages, I slid a digital recorder out of my pocket and set it on a statue's foot before switching it on. There wasn't much audio for it to capture, aside from the muted roar of the fire.

If nothing else, at least I'll be able to sell this as one of those white-noise sleep aids: The Soothing Sounds of China. The thought made me snicker.

It was strangely quiet here. I'd only been in the country three weeks, but I'd spent over a month in Indonesia last spring. There you could barely sleep, what with the frogs and crickets and everything else. Even the geckos sounded like a squeaky toy being strangled. It got really loud.

Yet when I returned to Minneapolis, where the night noises were courtesy of assholes with over-developed subwoofers, I missed it.

Either my hunger was playing tricks on me or the sausage was not too bad. It tasted like an ordinary hot dog, maybe a bit on the sweet side. I'm not sure if it was made out of penguins and corn, but apparently our beloved ballpark franks are made from lips and assholes, so who knows? Best not to think about it much.

The first can of Pringles opened with that satisfying pop I both knew and loved, and as I crunched a handful, I leaned against my statue buddy and tried to relax.

Something's bugging me.

Maybe it was leftover adrenaline from playing ninja in the temple, waiting for the moment Harold would notice I wasn't in the van, but I was wound tighter than a pissed-off terrier. If I couldn't get my nerves under control, this brilliant plan of mine was never gonna work. Cracking a Coke, I let the lukewarm acid fizz over my tongue, wishing I'd thought to bring some of rice wine along instead.

Feeling the urge to text Clarke, I pulled my phone from my pocket. As soon as I powered up, a dozen notifications made it ding like a slot machine: *ping ping ping ping!* The sound was ludicrously loud and somehow unwelcome, and my face burned as I put the phone on mute.

Clarke had been my best buddy since grade school, but he hadn't spoken to me in weeks. He was seriously pissed at me, and I knew why, but he'd never given me the silent treatment before. Even though I told myself not to get my hopes up, I couldn't help feeling optimistic. Sooner or later, he'd have to forgive me.

Sadly, aside from a single text from Roxi, the rest were from *her*.

I'd rather walk through fire than talk to *her*.

Still, call it boredom, call it masochism, but I glanced at one before I could stop myself.

I know u're mad, but u dont know my side.
Please talk to me, Jackson. I want to make this right.
Cant u see we need each other?
Especially now.
- B

I deleted the message before hitting the power button, watching as the screen went black.

A flicker of movement just outside the shelter made me look up. The skin on the back of my neck bristled.

Has that statue gotten closer?

It had been a lot farther away when I'd set up camp—I was sure of it.

That's ridiculous. Statues don't move.

Still, the way the light danced in the sculpture's eyes was unnerving.

A log cracked in the fire, startling me so I laughed out loud.

To think Roxi accused me of not having an imagination.

As it turned out, I might have had too much.

Made in the USA
Las Vegas, NV
15 December 2021

38025039R00062